The Boy
Who Made
The World
Disappear

Also by Ben Miller

The Night I Met Father Christmas

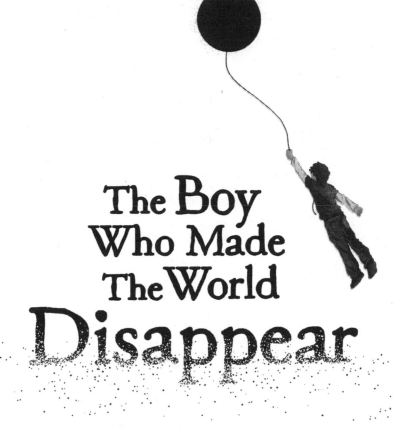

The Boy Who Made The World Disappear

BEN MILLER

with illustrations by Daniela Jaglenka Terrazzini

SIMON & SCHUSTER

First published in Great Britain in 2019 by Simon & Schuster UK Ltd

This paperback edition published 2020

7 9 10 8 6

Simon & Schuster UK Ltd
1st Floor, 222 Gray's Inn Road
London
WC1X 8HB

www.simonandschuster.co.uk
www.simonandschuster.com.au
www.simonandschuster.co.in

Simon & Schuster Australia, Sydney
Simon & Schuster India, New Delhi

A CIP catalogue record for this book is available from the British Library.

PB ISBN 978-1-4711-7267-0
eBook ISBN 978-1-4711-7268-7
Audio 978-1-4711-8548-9

Printed and bound by CPI Group (UK) Ltd, Croydon, CR0 4YY

To Stephen Hawking, who taught us all a thing
or two about black holes

brought his mother breakfast in bed and always shared his toys with his younger sister, Lana (despite the fact that she would often break them, lose them, or try to flush them down the loo). Harrison was kind to other children at school, even Hector Broom, who was a bit of a bully and once pushed Harrison over on purpose and then told their teacher, Miss Balogun, that it was an accident.

And Harrison was honest. If he broke a vase – for example, by accidentally knocking it off the shelf while pretending to be Bear Grylls – he would own up. He never stole from shops or cheated in Monopoly or snuck into the circus without paying. He tried every new food three times without complaint, always held a grown-up's hand when crossing the road and sometimes even folded his clothes at night instead of just chucking them on the floor.

Sometimes.

So, I hear you ask, if Harrison was so good, what Bad Thing could he possibly have done?

Well, you see, as kind and honest and good and big-hearted as he was, Harrison had a BIG flaw. He couldn't control his temper.

Most of the time, he was very well-behaved. But once in a while something would really annoy him. And then . . . well, then, he would Kick Off.

'*Euuurrgghhhh!*' Harrison would groan, in pure frustration. His head would lower, like a bull about to charge. His cheeks would redden, his brow would furrow, his eyes would narrow and he would clamp his jaws so tight it was a wonder he didn't snap a tooth.

'Code Red!' his father would cry, using his parents' nickname for Harrison's rages.

'DON'T SAY THAT!' Harrison would yell.

'Yes, definitely a Code Red,' his mother would agree, moving breakable objects to safety.

'AAAAARRRRRGGGGGHHHH!' Harrison would shout. 'I HATE IT WHEN YOU SAY THAT!'

From that point, there was very little anyone could do to calm Harrison down until he wore himself out.

'*EEUUURRRGH!*' he might exclaim, as he threw himself on the floor, kicking his legs, so that he went round and round in circles like a breakdancer.

'WHY WON'T ANYONE LISTEN

TO ME??!!' he might bawl, as he ran off into the undergrowth, punching the bushes in fury.

'I WANT A DIFFERENT FAMILY!!' he might roar, as he slammed the door to his room and barricaded it with every single one of his toys.

Now, usually Harrison's rages happened not because he was really cross, but because he was worried about something, which meant that most of the time, the grown-ups around him – his parents, for example, or his teachers – sort of understood. They'd wait out Harrison's meltdowns, then try to find out what he was really worried about so they could help him fix it. Then everything would go back to normal.

This story is *not* about one of those

would ask to join and then change the rules so Harrison couldn't play. Or, if they were playing football, he would trip Harrison up or push him off the ball.

But by far the worst thing was Hector's elastic band.

It was the perfect weapon: quick to use and easy to hide. When you were least expecting it, you'd feel the sharp sting of the elastic on your arm or your neck or your leg, and the next minute you'd be rolling around in pain.

Just the *thought* of having to go to Hector's party put Harrison on edge. But the whole class was going, and Harrison didn't want to be left out when everyone was talking about the party on Monday, so he had no choice.

The only thing that made going to Hector Broom's birthday remotely bearable was the theme: space. Because Harrison *loved* anything to do with stars and planets. Plus, Hector had been bragging all week that his parents had booked a real life astronaut as the entertainment. The astronaut's name was Shelley. She was staying with her grandmother, the school lollipop lady, for a special visit, so the Brooms had booked her immediately for their precious son's party.

Harrison couldn't wait to meet her. After all, she had actually been to space!

The party started happily enough. There were space decorations all over the village hall and Hector's mother and father had ordered a big birthday cake topped with a silver spaceship crashing into a red planet, next to a green alien with four eyes.

Everyone had come in fancy dress. Harrison

was a spaceman, Persephone Brinkwater was an alien, Charlie Nwosu had come as a shooting star, Marcus Down as a rocket and Carl Ng was a man from Mission Control. Katie Broad was an angel, but no one said anything, even though angels aren't the sort of thing you see in space.

Hector Broom had, predictably, chosen to dress as the Sun, because he wanted to come as the most important thing in our solar system.

Once the guests had arrived, Hector's parents ushered all the children to the centre of the room, and soon everyone was sitting on cushions on the floor, waiting impatiently for the main event.

Harrison could feel his excitement growing as the moment he would meet a real life astronaut grew closer.

Then a menacing voice whispered in his ear: 'Just wait until my parents are gone, I'm going to get you.' Harrison turned to see Hector Broom, flexing his dreaded elastic band, an evil glint in his eye. 'And when we start the games you'd better watch out!'

Harrison gulped. Perhaps he should have stayed at home after all.

The lights dimmed and a voice called out, 'Lift-off in T minus

ten . . . nine . . . eight . . . '

All the children began to join in.

'Seven . . . six . . . five . . . '

Hector's mother and father backed off towards the door. Harrison felt all his muscles go tense. Once they had gone, who was going to protect him from Hector?

'Four . . . three . . . two . . . one . . .

'Ignition! BLAST OFF!' yelled a woman, bursting out of the kitchen door.

She had bright pink hair and was wearing the most brilliant outfit, just like the ones the astronauts wear on the International Space Station. Despite his nerves, Harrison was really impressed.

'Hello, children! I'm Shelley, we're going to have so much fun together! Now, who wants to go up into space with me?' she asked, looking around.

'Me, me, me!' everyone shouted.

Hector's parents smiled at one another and closed the door. As soon as they had gone, Hector flashed Harrison an evil grin.

'Not me!' blurted Harrison.

'Excuse me?' asked Shelley, staring at Harrison in surprise.

'I want to go home!' Harrison cried, his panic at being pinged by Hector's elastic band growing.

'But, Harrison,' said Marcus Down, 'you love space.'

'No, I don't!' shouted Harrison. 'It's boring!'

Of course he didn't mean that at all, he was just scared of Hector. But Shelley didn't know that.

'Space isn't *boring*,' she replied firmly, with

a frown. 'In fact, you have no idea how lucky you are. When I was a little girl, I would have loved to go to a party like this.' She turned away from Harrison and addressed everyone else. 'Okay, children, lie down and close your eyes.'

Everyone did as they were told and, trying to ignore his worries, Harrison did the same.

With his eyes shut, he heard Shelley drawing the curtains and turning off the lights. There was a click, followed by a humming sound . . .

'Open your eyes!' Shelley instructed.

Harrison did, and suddenly it was as if they were all floating in space! There were stars everywhere! Swirling on the ceiling, covering the walls and falling to the ground.

'Who knows what a constellation is?'

Shelley asked. Harrison put his hand up, but Shelley picked Persephone Brinkwater instead.

'Stars that make a shape,' said Persephone.

'Very good,' said Shelley. 'Now, everyone look up and meet the Great Bear.' She directed a laser pointer at the ceiling so that a bright red dot circled several stars which – it had to be said – looked nothing like a bear.

'There's its head,' explained Shelley, as the dot danced above them. 'There are its paws, there's its body and those are its legs.'

'If you say so,' said Carl Ng, and several of the children giggled.

'Can anyone guess what this constellation is?' said Shelley, sounding slightly irritated. Her laser moved to another cluster of stars.

Yet again, Harrison put his hand up.

Shelley pointed to Charlie Nwosu.

'Is it a bat?' asked Charlie.

'Not quite,' replied Shelley. 'Though it does have wings. This is Cygnus, the swan. It's one of my favourites. Can any of you guess why?'

'Because it has a very bright star in it?' asked Hector Broom, without even putting his hand up.

'Really good guess, Hector,' said Shelley. 'What a clever boy you are. And it *is* a very bright star. It's called *Deneb*, which means tail in Arabic, because it's in the tail of the swan. But the reason Cygnus is one my favourite constellations is right here . . .' She took the laser pointer, and squiggled it in a dark bit right in the middle of the swan. 'It's a black hole. Does anyone know what one of those is?'

Harrison, who knew all about black holes, sat up in excitement and waved both arms. 'I do!' he said. 'I do!'

'No one?' said Shelley, pretending not to hear. After his outburst, she had decided that Harrison was a spoilt boy who needed to be taught a lesson. 'Well, it's basically a hole in the universe. It's completely black, so you'd never know it was there. But if you get too close, it will suck you inside and you will disappear for ever.'

As she spoke, she switched off the laser pointer and the little point of red light on the ceiling suddenly vanished.

There was a pause. The children stared at the little patch of sky where the black hole was lurking, feeling slightly freaked out.

'Right!' said Shelley, climbing to her feet. 'Shall we play some games?' She flicked a row of switches on the wall, and the lights came back on.

'No!' shouted Harrison. The other children had all stood up, but he was still lying on the floor.

'Excuse me?' said Shelley.

'I don't want to play games!' he cried. Suddenly, the only thing he could think about was Hector's elastic band.

'But they're space games,' said Shelley, taken aback. 'You'll love them. We've got Accrete the Neutron Star, that's like Pass the Parcel. Sleeping Supernovas, which is a bit like Sleeping Lions—'

'I love Sleeping Lions!' cried Katie Broad.

'*AAAAAARRRRRRGGGGGGHHHHH!*'

cried Harrison. 'Why isn't anyone listening to me?!'

'Harrison,' said Shelley, a note of warning in her voice. 'I think you need to calm down.'

'I want to see the stars again!' he yelled.

'We're finished with the stars,' said Shelley firmly. 'Now we're going to play games. Shall we start with a round of Pin the Satellite into Low Earth Orbit? Hector, you can go first.'

Hector stepped forward and, unnoticed by Shelley, he pulled his rubber band out of his pocket and aimed a menacing smirk at Harrison.

Which was when Harrison really flew into a rage.

'THIS IS THE WORST PARTY EVER!' he hullaballooed, running around the room, kicking the cushions like footballs. 'AND YOU'RE A RUBBISH ASTRONAUT!'

'Now wait a minute,' said Shelley, getting increasingly cross herself.

'I HATE YOU!' Harrison barked. 'I WISH I COULD PUT *YOU* IN THE BLACK HOLE! I WISH I COULD PUT *EVERYTHING* INTO A BLACK HOLE!'

'LIKE I CARE!' bellowed Shelley at the top of her voice.

Harrison was so surprised to be yelled at that he stopped in his tracks.

'YOU THINK I WANT TO DO THIS?' howled Shelley. 'YOU THINK I WANT TO BE A PRETEND ASTRONAUT? I WANT TO BE AN ASTRONOMER, NOT A

CHILDREN'S ENTERTAINER!'

Silence fell in the room, as the children sat with open mouths. Shelley wasn't acting like grown-ups were supposed to at all!

'You're not a real astronaut?' asked Marcus Down.

'OF COURSE I'M NOT!' cried Shelley. 'JUST LIKE YOU'RE NOT REAL ROCKETS, PLANETS, STARS OR . . . ANGELS!'

Katie Broad started to cry.

'Okay! Okay!' said Shelley, realising that the situation was growing out of control. 'I'm sorry. Just . . . I've been through a lot recently.'

Persephone Brinkwater put her arm round Katie Broad, who was still wailing.

Shelley took a deep breath and started

again. 'Come on, let's play some fun games,' she said, acting as if nothing had happened at all. 'And ... then we can all have some delicious birthday cake.'

Of course the party never really recovered. They did play Pin the Satellite into Low Earth Orbit, but Harrison punctured the International Space Station and got disqualified. Then they played Accrete the Neutron Star and everyone won a toy except for Harrison. Finally they played Sleeping Supernovas and Shelley caught Harrison scratching his eczema rather than lying still so she exploded him and he had to sit out for the rest of the game.

All the while, Hector Broom snapped his rubber band with a threatening glare.

By the time they were ready for their food,

Harrison was in a Very Bad Mood. And then things went from worse to disastrous.

'Harrison! I'm sorry, but you can't have any,' called Shelley, as all the kids grabbed a slice of birthday cake.

'Why not?' said Harrison, watching the others tuck into the delicious-looking cake.

'Katie says you're allergic to dairy,' Shelley said. 'And this cake isn't dairy-free so no cake for you.'

'Well, I'm eating it!' said Harrison, grabbing a chunk of cake.

'No, you're not!' said Shelley. 'Step away from the cake!'

'OWWW!' cried Harrison. His neck was suddenly red hot! He spun round to see Hector. He had pinged Harrison with his elastic band!

'Is everything okay in here?' said Hector's mum, interrupting the scene. Harrison looked up to see Hector's parents standing at the door. Through the window, Harrison could see the other parents arriving too.

'Oh, yes, fine. Everything's fine, isn't it, children?' said Shelley. Her cheeks bloomed red, but Hector's mum didn't seem to notice.

'Did you enjoy the party?' Harrison's mother asked him as she walked over.

Harrison looked at Shelley, then at Hector Broom, then back at his parents. Should he tell, or not?

'Yes, I did,' he nodded, crossing his fingers behind his back.

Hector's mother clapped her hands. 'Thank you all for coming to celebrate our dear little angel's birthday. I'm afraid it's time for everyone to go home now, but I think we might have some very special balloons for everyone to take with them, and a party bag too! Shelley?'

'Of course,' said Shelley.

One by one, Shelley gave each child a party bag and a beautiful, shiny helium balloon in the shape of a planet. There was a stripy brown and yellow Jupiter for Hector Broom and a purple Venus for Persephone Brinkwater. Charlie Nwosu got a sky-blue Neptune, Marcus Down an orange Saturn with pink rings and Carl Ng a bluey-green Uranus. Katie Broad got a silvery Mercury, which was very lucky because it matched her angel costume.

Finally, it was Harrison's turn.

'Have you got a balloon for Harrison?' his

mother asked Shelley.

'Oh, yes,' said Shelley. Something flickered in her eyes. 'I've got a very special balloon for Harrison. Just wait here one minute.'

She disappeared into the kitchen, closing the door behind her.

'What was your favourite bit of the party?' asked Harrison's father.

'When we saw the black hole,' said Harrison.

The sound of banging came from the kitchen.

'What's a black hole?' asked his mother.

'It's a hole in the universe,' said Harrison. 'They're very dangerous, because if you fall inside one, you'll never get out.'

'What do they look like?'

'Like a hole,' said Harrison. 'That's black.'

There was a whizzing sound from the kitchen, as if something was being put in a blender. Then . . .

BANG!

The kitchen door blew clean off its hinges, sailed across the hall, slammed against the opposite wall and clattered onto the floor.

There, framed in the doorway, was Shelley. Her space suit was covered in soot and all her pink hair was on end. In her right hand was a piece of string, and floating at the end of it was a weird black circle.

'Um . . . are you okay?' asked Harrison's father.

'Here's your balloon, Harrison,' said Shelley, tying the string to his wrist.

'That's very kind of you,' said Harrison's mother.

'My pleasure' said Shelley. 'He deserves it.'

Harrison reached out his hand, took hold of the string and pulled the balloon towards him. It was pitch black, like a piece had been cut out of the universe. He blew at it, to see if it bobbed backwards like a balloon should, but instead it loomed ever so slightly closer.

'I wouldn't do that, if I were you,' Shelley warned. 'In fact, best not to touch it.'

Harrison's father gave her a quizzical look.

'In case it pops,' said Shelley, smiling a big, innocent smile.

'Well? What do you say, Harrison?' asked his mother.

'Thank you,' said Harrison politely.

'You're most welcome, Harrison,' said Shelley with a glint in her eye. 'You are most welcome indeed.'

Harrison reached out his hand, took hold of the string
and pulled the balloon towards him.

Chapter Two

As Harrison walked home with his parents, he studied his extraordinary balloon. In fact, he couldn't take his eyes off it. He was vaguely aware of crossing the village green and climbing the hill to their cottage, but it was as if it was all happening to someone else. The balloon was like a huge dark magnet, pulling him in. He stared deeper and deeper into its depths, looking for a place to rest his eyes: a shape, maybe, moving in the black, or a tiny chink of light. But there was nothing. Harrison was starting to wonder if it even was a balloon, or something altogether more mysterious . . .

'*RUFF!*'

A loud bark startled Harrison from his thoughts as a set of sharp white fangs snapped shut about a centimetre from the end of his nose. He leapt in fright, letting go of the string. Luckily, the balloon was tied to his wrist, otherwise it would have floated away and, well, this would pretty much be the end of the story.

Harrison knew that terrifying bark and those razor-sharp teeth all too well.

They belonged to Blue, his neighbour Mr Hardwick's black-and-white Border Collie. His heart began to race and he started to feel faint.

'Help!' he cried.

'Just turn your back, Harrison,' said Mr Hardwick, leaning over the fence. 'Blue won't hurt you. Stand still and she'll soon lose interest.'

Harrison did as Mr Hardwick suggested and turned away from the dog. Then he felt Blue's hot breath on his neck as she snapped her teeth just millimetres from his right ear lobe. He turned back around and tried to shoo the dog away.

'Don't wave your arms,' said his mother calmly. 'She thinks you want to play.'

Harrison held his arms close to his chest.

He could feel his heart thumping against his ribs, like a crazed hamster trying to break out of a cage. Blue darted in front of him and kept jumping up, barking and snapping her teeth in his face. It was unbearable.

'*Agghhh!*' yelled Harrison.

'Oh, don't be so silly, Harrison,' said his father. 'Blue's just being friendly.'

The next few seconds felt like hours. As his parents continued their conversation with Mr Hardwick, Harrison twisted and turned, doing everything he could to avoid Blue's yapping and snapping. But the dog wasn't giving up, this was much too fun a game.

She crouched low on the pavement . . .

Prepared to leap . . .

Sprang from the ground . . .

Harrison shut his eyes tight and ducked!

For the longest time, he stayed in that position with his eyes closed, expecting to be torn apart at any moment. But nothing happened.

He opened his eyes.

'They left our recycling box behind,' Harrison's mother was saying.

'Because we put a soggy

tissue in it. I thought paper was recyclable?'

Harrison looked up and down the lane. Blue was nowhere to be seen.

'That's the council for you,' Mr Hardwick replied. 'They love to make things difficult.'

Where had the dog gone? Harrison couldn't make any sense of it.

And then he remembered he was still holding his balloon. His very strange balloon . . .

It couldn't have anything to do with the dog disappearing, could it?

He crouched down, just like he had when Blue had sprung at him, and looked up. As he suspected, the balloon was hovering directly above him. So when Blue had leapt for him, she could easily have hit it. What if she had crashed *into* the blackness and vanished?

Harrison shook his head. No, that was ridiculous. Blue must have jumped right over him and run off down the street while he had his eyes shut. Perhaps she'd seen a squirrel and run after it or heard a cat wailing down on the village green?

'Harrison, are you all right?' his father asked.

Harrison didn't say anything. His mind was whirring with possibilities. Could Blue have really disappeared into the balloon? And if so, did that mean he could make other things disappear?

Chapter Three

As soon as Harrison was safely inside his bedroom, he set to work.

First, he tested what would happen when he let go of the balloon's string. Cautiously, he untied the knot round his wrist. Instead of floating up to the ceiling like a normal helium balloon would do, it hovered mysteriously in mid-air. Harrison was tempted to poke it with his finger, but Shelley's warning not to touch it rang in his ears. If it really could swallow a medium-sized Border Collie, what could it do to him?

He walked around the balloon so he could look at it from every possible angle. He crouched down and gazed up at it, and stood up on tiptoe, peering down. It looked exactly the same from every direction: a flat black circle. Like a piece of black card had been cut out and stuck in mid-air. It wasn't round like a balloon should be.

He noticed it didn't have a knot either. Whenever he got a balloon from a fair or a party, there was always a knot at the bottom where the string was attached. But this thing, whatever it was, didn't have one. Instead, the string just sort of vanished into the blackness.

Hmmm . . . Harrison was starting to have an idea of what his 'balloon' might really be.

He closed his bedroom curtains, switched on his torch and turned out the lights. He swished the beam around in the darkness, until he found the 'balloon'. Which was when he noticed the oddest thing. Instead of reflecting off the surface, the torch beam seemed to disappear right into it. Harrison shone the torch onto a bowling ball sitting on his shelf, so he could compare the two. But that looked round and shiny and – quite frankly – like a ball. Not flat and completely black.

Harrison turned the light back on and then crawled under his bed, rummaging around until he found the toy he was looking for: a fluffy grey elephant called Elmond. He and

Chapter Four

The next day was a school day and Harrison's alarm woke him with a start.

Beep! Beep! Beep!

For an awful moment, he wondered whether the black hole might have been a dream. But, to his great relief, when he sat up and opened his eyes, there it was, tied to the bottom of the bed exactly where he had left it.

Was it smaller than it had been the night before? Or was he imagining things?

All balloons shrink a bit overnight, he reassured himself. Maybe black holes were no different? Either way, today he was going to have some fun.

Beep! Beep! Beep!

He picked up his alarm clock from his bedside table and launched it through the air!

Beep! Beep! Bee—yowp!

The clock had an irritating smiley-face sun on it and Harrison watched with satisfaction as it faded from view.

Oh, yes, this was going to be a great day.

It was their father's turn to walk Harrison and Lana down the hill to school. Luckily, he was so busy doing whatever it is that grown-ups do on their phones that he didn't notice Harrison had brought his black hole. He also didn't notice when Harrison took his reading book from his satchel and threw it over his shoulder. And he most definitely didn't notice when that self-same reading book froze at the surface of the black hole and slowly faded from view.

Ha! thought Harrison. *Now no one will know I didn't do my reading homework!*

Harrison smiled to himself. His black hole was primed and ready for action.

Soon they reached the bottom of the hill, where a crowd of parents and schoolchildren was hovering near Shelley's grandmother, the school lollipop lady.

Now, I need to give you a bit of background on Shelley's grandmother. As I've already mentioned, she was the school lollipop lady, meaning she helped all the children and parents cross the busy road outside the school. Secondly, she was known to be slightly strange. Very few cars came through the village, so you might think she would be constantly leading children across the road, but that wasn't how she operated at all.

Instead, every morning, she would wait with her lollipop until a large crowd had gathered round her. The road would be empty, without a car to be seen. But would she cross? Oh, no. She would wait. And wait. Then, as soon as she saw a car coming, she would inch her way into the middle of the road, plant her pole and blow her whistle.

Once, when there was a very long gap between cars, one of the fathers had grown impatient, taken his children by the hand and started to cross the road without her permission.

PHEEEEEP!

He stopped in his tracks.

'There's nothing coming!' he exclaimed.

PHEEEEEP! went Shelley's grandmother's whistle.

'But—'

PHEEEEEEP!

'I—'

PHEEEEEEEP!

Luckily, at that moment an elderly cyclist had pootled into view, so Shelley's grandmother was able to voyage to the middle of the road, plant her pole and let everyone cross.

Usually the lollipop lady wasn't one for conversation, so Harrison was very surprised when she smiled as he approached and put a friendly hand on his shoulder.

'Ah, you must be Harrison,' she said, with a twinkle in her eye. 'What did you think of Hector's birthday party?'

'It was okay,' said Harrison. 'But I had an argument with your granddaughter. She wasn't very nice to me.'

'Ah, is that so? Did she give you that balloon?' she asked innocently, pointing at the black hole. 'It's a very unusual colour.'

'Yes,' replied Harrison carefully. Could Shelley's grandmother know the truth about his 'balloon'?

'Have you put anything in it yet?' whispered Shelley's grandmother, leaning in close so no one else could hear.

So she *did* know! Which meant that Shelley must have intentionally given him the black hole . . . but why? Harrison checked to see if his father was listening, but he seemed to be busy chatting away on his phone. 'Only Elmond the elephant. And some broccoli,' Harrison whispered. 'And my alarm clock. And my reading book.'

'Your secret's safe with me,' said Shelley's grandmother, tapping her nose. 'But be careful. Once you put something in there, it can never come out.'

'That's okay,' said Harrison. 'I don't want that stuff back.'

'Are you a witch?' interrupted Lana. It

was a bit rude, but Harrison knew what she meant. The lollipop lady didn't have warts or a cloak or a black cat, but there was something ever so slightly unusual about her. Maybe it was her sharp green eyes . . .

'Quite the opposite, my dear,' Shelley's grandmother replied. 'I'm training to become an astronomer.' Both Lana and Harrison looked impressed.

'Like Shelley?' asked Harrison.

'Very like Shelley. In fact, exactly like Shelley,' said Shelley's grandmother, chuckling. 'And this must be your father.'

Their father, who was still busy on his phone, nodded hello.

'Or, of course, it could be you, Harrison,' said Shelley's grandmother. 'Only older.'

'Me?' asked Harrison.

'Have you never thought,' replied the old lady, 'that if you want to know what you will look like when you grow up, you should look at your parents?'

Harrison hadn't.

'Or your grandparents,' added Shelley's grandmother, rather mischievously. Then, seeing that Harrison's father was still on his phone, and not really listening, she said in a low voice, 'You must keep feeding it, you know.'

'Feeding it?' asked Harrison in the quietest voice he could manage.

'Or it will shrink to nothing. That's the thing about black holes,' said Shelley's grandmother. 'Always hungry.'

'*I'm* hungry,' said Lana. 'I want some cake.'

'No one's having any cake,' said Harrison's

father, ending his call. 'You've only just had breakfast. And, besides, Harrison's got swimming.'

Swimming!

Harrison had completely forgotten. Monday was swimming day!

Which reminds me: there's something else I need to tell you about Harrison. He wasn't in any way a scaredy-cat, but like most people, there were some things that he Didn't Like At All. You might be scared of spiders or dentists or mouldy grapes, for example. But Harrison? Well, for Harrison, it was swimming.

It had all started with his very first lesson. His father had taken him to the local pool, where a large, round-faced man with curly hair told him that he was his new swimming instructor and would have him water-borne in no time.

'Let's see what you can do, Harrison,' said the instructor, as he removed Harrison's armbands.

'I can sink,' said Harrison. 'But that's about it.'

'Swimming is all in the mind,' the instructor told him. 'If you think you can't do it, you can't. If you think you can –' he smiled a knowing smile – 'you might surprise yourself.'

'What if I surprise myself by drowning?' Harrison had asked.

'You won't drown,' the instructor had said with a chuckle. 'I'll be right here the whole time.'

Of course, what the curly-haired instructor

hadn't known when he'd said that was that there would be a lady instructor in the pool that morning, and that the two of them would really enjoy chatting. In fact, they would enjoy chatting so much that when Harrison did need help and began to splutter and swallow and sink beneath the water, the curly-haired swimming instructor would completely fail to notice. It was only when Harrison tugged at the curly-haired instructor's shorts to get his attention, accidentally pulling them down, that the man finally realised what was happening. Even then, he seemed to be crosser that the lady instructor saw his bottom than sorry that Harrison had nearly drowned.

Ever since, Harrison had a huge fear of water. So, when Harrison's father mentioned swimming, I think you can guess what happened. Harrison started to lose it.

'No!' he exclaimed, throwing his school bag on the pavement. 'I'm not going!'

'Harrison,' said his father patiently, 'you can't keep doing this, week after week. Everyone has to learn to swim.'

'I haven't got my swimming kit!' said Harrison.

'Oh, that's all right,' his father said. 'I'm sure the school will have some spare shorts.'

'The spare shorts are too big!' exclaimed Harrison. 'They'll soak up loads of water and drag me under and I'll drown!'

'Enough, Harrison,' said his father in a firm voice. 'You're going swimming and that's final.'

'*Euuurrgghhhhh!*' groaned Harrison. 'It's

not fair!' And with that, he lowered his head, furrowed his brow, narrowed his eyes and ground his teeth.

'Uh-oh,' said Harrison's father. 'Code Red Alert.'

'DON'T SAY THAT!' shouted Harrison. 'I HATE IT WHEN YOU SAY THAT!'

The crowd around them began to move back.

'*EEUUURRRGH!*' cried Harrison, kicking his legs.

'Over to you,' said Shelley's grandmother to Harrison's father, with a grin. 'Duty calls.'

Sure enough, putt-putt-putting up the road was a very old man on a tiny electric scooter. Shelley's grandmother inched forward onto the tarmac and planted her lollipop pole, forcing him to screech to a halt. The waiting crowd surged across the road and in through the school gates.

'Harrison, come on, we'll be late,' said his father.

'I'M *NOT* GOING SWIMMING!!' roared Harrison. 'AND YOU CAN'T MAKE ME!'

Forty-five minutes later, in a Deeply Upsetting Turn of Events, Harrison found himself sitting on a wooden bench in the boys' changing room, wearing a very large pair of grey swimming trunks from the spares box.

'Harrison, are you still in there?' called

Miss Balogun from the other side of the door. 'I've forgotten my goggles, so I'm just going back to the girls' changing room. We'll start your lesson when I get back. Alfie Bone has joined the Big Swimmers this week, so you're the only Beginner, which means I'll be able to give you lots of attention!'

The only Beginner. That didn't sound like much fun. How Harrison longed to be like the other children, laughing and splashing and jumping in the big pool! Instead, he'd be on his own with Miss Balogun in the shallow pool, sinking and spluttering and swallowing a lot of water. If only he could swallow enough to drain the entire pool! Then he wouldn't have to swim at all.

Which was when he had an idea . . .

After tying a bow in the drawstring of his

much-too-big shorts so that they didn't fall down, Harrison opened the locker where he had hidden his black hole.

It's definitely getting smaller, he thought to himself. *There's no way it could have fitted in there last night. Shelley's grandmother was right, it needs feeding.*

Then he remembered Miss Balogun might return at any moment, so he had to work fast.

With the black hole bobbing behind him, he swished through the footbath and into the pool area. To his left, through the glass that separated the shallow and deep pools, he saw all the other children in his class, laughing and playing in the big pool. As he watched, Hector Broom (who as usual was wearing a fancy swimming cap with a number one on it) ran to the end of a very bouncy diving board and belly-flopped into the water. *Show-off,* thought Harrison. He looked to his right. The shallow pool was completely empty.

Making sure the coast was clear, Harrison tiptoed towards the shallow pool, his black hole floating behind him. He walked down the steps into the water, guiding the black hole carefully. He was three steps down when he realised he was making a terrible mistake. If he was in the water when the black hole touched it, he might get dragged in too, like a spider being sucked down a plughole. Somehow, he had to find a way of getting the black hole to touch the water while he wasn't in it.

Which was when he spotted the lifeguard hook lying by the side of the pool.

Perhaps you've seen these at the swimming pool? It's basically a long pole, with a hook on the end. The idea is that if someone in the pool needs help, the lifeguard can hook them to safety, and they are especially handy if you happen to be a lifeguard who doesn't like getting their clothes wet.

It was the work of a moment for Harrison to tie the black hole to the end of the pole, and the work of several minutes for him to lift it at its middle, balance it on his chest like a tightrope walker, shuffle to the edge of the pool and hold it out so the black hole was suspended over the water. Finally, he tipped the pole so that the hook sank beneath the surface, pulling the black hole with it.

Which is when an extraordinary thing happened. As the black hole descended, the water below it rose up like a fountain, higher and higher, as if being sucked upwards, until finally it touched the edge of the hole.

A split-second later, there was the most enormous bang, and Harrison shut his eyes as spray showered in all directions!

When he opened them again, he was completely surrounded by thick white fog.

PHEEEEEEEP! sounded a whistle.

Harrison couldn't see a thing, but he could hear the excited chatter of children's voices.

'WHAT'S GOING ON?!' he heard Miss Balogun shout. 'Harrison? Are you in there?'

Ever so slowly, the fog began to clear. The glass wall that separated the shallow pool from the big pool was filled with children's faces pressed against it. Behind them, Miss Balogun was standing with her mouth wide open at the scene before her.

The glass wall that separated the shallow pool from the big pool was filled with children's faces pressed against it.

All the water had completely disappeared and, standing on the wet tiles, in the middle of an empty pool, was Harrison, making swimming movements.

'I think I'm getting the hang of this,' he called out in a cheerful voice.

Which was when his shorts fell down.

Chapter Five

'**I**'m really sorry, Harrison,' said Miss Balogun, still sounding in shock. 'But it looks like you're going to have to miss your swimming lesson.'

'That's okay,' said Harrison, trying to look sad but secretly jumping for joy.

They were back in the changing room, while all the other children carried on their lesson. Miss Balogun had called 999, but when the man on the end of the phone asked, 'Which service?' she found it very hard to decide. There wasn't a fire, so she didn't need a fire engine, and no one had committed a crime, so there was no point informing the police. She thought about calling an ambulance, but Harrison insisted he was absolutely fine. To make matters worse, when she tried to explain to the man from 999 that all the water in the shallow swimming pool had vanished into thin air, he thought she was making a prank call, and got very cross and hung up.

'So one minute the water was there,' Miss Balogun said to Harrison, 'and the next, it disappeared?'

Harrison nodded.

'I think what happened,' said Miss Balogun, trying to make sense of it all, 'is there must have been a leak.'

'Yes,' said Harrison.

'I mean . . . water doesn't just disappear, docs it?' said Miss Balogun.

'No,' said Harrison.

'Maybe the caretaker emptied it for cleaning and didn't tell us?'

'Almost definitely,' said Harrison. He felt mean for tricking his teacher, but it was either that or get into a lot of trouble and possibly get his black hole confiscated.

'And you're definitely okay?' asked Miss Balogun.

'One hundred per cent,' Harrison replied.

'Okay,' said Miss Balogun, happier

now that she had decided on some sort of explanation. 'Why don't we both get changed and have a hot chocolate while we wait for the rest of the class?'

To Harrison's great joy, that's exactly what they did. And Harrison was not only allowed a hot chocolate (dairy-free, of course), but a packet of crisps as well, in his favourite flavour, salt and vinegar.

And while they waited, Miss Balogun called the council and complained about the shallow pool being emptied without any notice, which seemed to make her feel much better.

Harrison stared lovingly at his black hole. The two of them were going to have so much fun together. Now that it had drunk all that water, it was back to its normal size. Shelley's grandmother had been right, it really did need feeding.

The first opportunity for Harrison to feed the hole again came almost immediately. Harrison (like most of you, I'm sure) was not a big fan of school food, and on the menu that lunchtime was liver and onions. *Yuk!* To make matters worse, that week Hector Broom was Handy Helper. Handy Helpers got to wear a crown, help Miss Balogun in the classroom and have an extra biscuit at afternoon break. They also served the food out to everyone else at lunchtime.

Hector had been Handy Helper before;

in fact, he had been chosen lots and lots of times. And Hector being in charge at lunchtime meant that if there was something tasty on the menu then Harrison would get hardly any, and if there was something horrible, Hector Broom would make sure Harrison got the biggest portion in the tin.

As you might expect, when the tin arrived at the table, Hector Broom gave himself a tiny little piece of liver and gave Harrison one that was GIANT.

'Do you want some onions?' asked Hector.

'No, thank you,' said Harrison.

Of course, Hector Broom didn't listen and dished out half a bucketful. Then he served all the other children on the table, giving them big pieces of liver too. He gave everyone a tiny spoonful of mashed potato, and himself a whole heap.

So you can imagine how surprised Hector was when, barely a minute later, Harrison pushed forward his empty plate and licked his lips.

'Mmmm,' Harrison said. 'Thank you, Hector. That was absolutely delicious.'

Of course, Harrison had hidden his black hole down by his feet, and what Hector Broom didn't see was Harrison's uneaten lunch, slowly fading to nothing on its surface.

'Oh, you liked it, did you?' Hector said, with a sneer. 'Well, there's an extra bit of liver here. You can have that too.'

He put another HUGE piece on Harrison's plate.

Harrison waited until Hector wasn't

looking, then dumped the liver in his black hole, and once again pushed forward his empty plate.

'Yum!' said Harrison. 'Thank you, that was delicious!'

The other children at the table laughed, which made Hector Broom – who always liked to be the boss – very cross indeed.

'I see,' he said. 'Then you can eat all of ours too!'

And, thinking he was being really mean, Hector Broom took his serving spoon and piled all of everyone else's portions onto Harrison's plate. Then he took his own tiny morsel and arranged it on top.

'Happy eating, Liver Boy,' said Hector Broom with a smile.

'Oh, is that all?' asked Harrison. 'You

haven't got any more, have you?'

The other children laughed again, and Hector Broom got even more angry.

'Shut up!' he hissed at them. 'It's not funny!'

'Look!' said Harrison, pointing. 'It's crumble for pudding!'

While Hector was distracted, Harrison tipped his entire plate into the black hole, then pushed it forward, completely empty.

'Finished!' he announced. The other children started laughing and clapping.

Hector Broom narrowed his eyes.

'Cheat!' he growled. 'You threw it all on the floor!' He stormed round to where Harrison was sitting, expecting to see a pile of discarded liver. But, of course, all he saw was Harrison's black hole.

'Where did it go? And what's this?' he asked, pointing at the black hole.

'Careful!' said Harrison. 'It's my balloon. From your party. Don't touch it!'

'What a baby!' cooed Hector. 'Bringing his balloon to school!'

The other children laughed, and Harrison felt his ears go hot.

Then Hector Broom took out his elastic band and flexed it menacingly. 'You wait,' he said, an evil glint in his eye. 'I'm going to get you. No one makes a fool of me.'

Sure enough, the showdown with Hector Broom happened straight after lunch.

Harrison was in the middle of a game of Cops and Robbers with his friends when he felt a tap on his shoulder. He turned to see Hector Broom, flanked by two bigger boys from the year above. He just had time to grab his black hole before the two boys hoisted him up by his armpits and carried him across the playground, then dumped him down behind the bike shed.

'Think you're clever, do you, Liver Boy?' snarled Hector.

Behind the bike shed was Hector Broom's favourite place to bring his victims. It was completely hidden from the teachers and so the perfect place for him to wield his elastic band. Harrison knew he had to act fast.

'Leave me alone, Hector!' he shouted,

hoping someone might hear him and come to his rescue.

'*Ssssshhhh*,' whispered Hector Broom, and stroked Harrison's hair, like a villain in a movie. 'One more word and Biter –' he pulled out his elastic band, ready to strike – 'will have something to say about it!'

'No one can see you here, squirt,' said one of the bigger boys.

'It's very secluded,' said the other. 'That's a Year Five word.'

'It means no one can see us,' clarified the first bigger boy, looking smug.

'Oh, yes, they can!' shouted Harrison, and swung his black hole at the metal wall of the bike shed.

What happened next was extraordinary.

The entire bike shed, and all the bikes in it,

crumpled into nothing, shooting off into the black hole. It was like that trick magicians do, where they pull a string of hankies out of their sleeve, only in reverse. A split-second later, all that was left at the edge of the black hole was the handlebars of a bicycle, slowly fading from view.

Hector Broom and the two bigger boys couldn't believe their eyes.

'What's going on?' asked Hector.

'My bike's gone!' said one of the bigger boys.

'It's an illusion, like on *Britain's Got Talent*!' said the other.

Over by the school, the teacher on duty, Mr Yeabsley, looked up to see what the commotion was. He scratched his head. Hadn't there been a bike shed there a minute ago?

Now that Mr Yeabsley and the whole school yard could see him, Hector Broom didn't dare ping Harrison with his elastic band, in case he got caught.

'Did you say you got that at my party?' he asked Harrison, pointing to the black hole. 'I only got a lousy brown one and it's already gone flat.'

Harrison nodded.

'I'll trade you for it,' said Hector Broom.

'No,' Harrison said in the bravest voice he could manage. 'I don't want to trade.' Hector had made him trade so many things he had loved – his fossils, his crystals, his Pokemon cards – but his black hole was one thing he wasn't giving to Hector for anything.

Hector Broom glanced across at Mr

Yeabsley, who was staring straight at them.

'Fine. Then I'll just take it. It was my birthday, I should have had the best balloon!' said Hector, and snatched hold of the string.

'No!' shouted Harrison, holding on as tight as he could.

The two bigger boys looked at each other. They wanted to help Hector, but now that they didn't have the bike shed to hide behind, they were worried about getting caught.

'Let go!' hissed Hector in Harrison's ear.

'Never!' said Harrison, pulling with all his might. 'It's mine!'

'Have it, then!' said Hector, and let go. Harrison tumbled to the ground, still holding on tight to the string.

For a few seconds, Harrison just sat there, panting.

'Oi!' shouted Mr Yeabsley. 'What's going on?'

'Nothing, sir!' Hector called back, with a smile, then he held out his hand to Harrison. 'I'm *so* sorry,' he said. 'Let me help you up.'

'Good boy, Hector!' called Mr Yeabsley.

But of course Hector didn't help Harrison up. Instead, as soon as the teacher wasn't looking, he aimed 'Biter' at Harrison's left earlobe.

'Oww!' yelped Harrison and let go of the black hole.

'Thank you very much,' said Hector Broom, grabbing the string and admiring his new toy. 'How do you think it works?' he asked the two bigger boys, stretching out a pudgy finger.

'Don't touch it!' blurted Harrison. 'It's

not really a balloon, it's a black hole! It'll suck you in and you'll never be able to get out again!'

'Forget it, Liver Boy,' said Hector Broom, with a snarl. 'I'm not falling for any more of your tri—'

But that was as much as he got to say, because at that very instant, Hector Broom touched the edge of the black hole and shot inside, like a boy falling head first through an open manhole. One minute he was there, the next all that could be seen was the soles of his shoes fading slowly from view.

Chapter Six

'Hector Broom?' Miss Balogun called, taking the register after lunch.

No one replied.

'Has anyone seen Hector?' asked Miss Balogun, peering over at Hector Broom's empty desk.

Harrison snuck a guilty glance at his black

hole, floating beside him. If anything, it was now slightly larger than when Shelley had given it to him. He wondered if he should say something to Miss Balogun. But who was going to believe him if he said Hector Broom had disappeared into a black hole?

'No?' asked their teacher one more time. 'Well,' said Miss Balogun, 'perhaps he's gone home. I'll check with the school secretary. In any case, someone else had better be Handy Helper. Harrison, as you had to miss out on swimming this morning, would you like to help me?'

Harrison couldn't help but grin. He had always wanted to be Handy Helper!

'Oh, yes, please,' he said, and walked to the front of the class. Miss Balogun picked up the Handy Helper crown from her desk and placed it on Harrison's head. It fitted perfectly.

'Right, well, for starters could you please go to the cupboard and take out the geography textbooks?' asked Miss Balogun. 'We're going to learn about waste management, and then we're going to have a test on it.'

'Oh!' moaned all the children. Geography was not their favourite subject.

'Perhaps everyone would rather do French instead?' asked Miss Balogun, knowing full well that French was the only subject worse than geography.

'Geography!' came the reply.

'Geography it is, then,' said Miss Balogun, handing Harrison the key to the store cupboard.

'But . . .' said Harrison. 'But . . .'

He was starting to feel extremely anxious. He hated tests!

'Yes, Harrison?' asked Miss Balogun.

'I-I'm,' stuttered Harrison, trying really hard not to lose his cool.

'I DON'T WANT TO DO A TEST!' was what he *wanted* to shout, closely followed by, 'GO AND GET THE BOOKS YOURSELF!' But he figured that might get him into all sorts of trouble.

He caught sight of the black hole, peeping out from behind his desk.

Of course! He didn't need to lose his temper! He could use the black hole instead!

'I'LL GO AND DO THAT FOR YOU RIGHT NOW!' he said in a bit of a shouty voice, because he was still quite worked up.

'Right,' said Miss Balogun, slightly confused as to why Harrison was speaking so loudly. 'Thank you.'

As calmly as he could, Harrison walked past his desk, making sure to pick up his black hole, and out to the cupboard in the corridor.

Just a few seconds later, he returned.

'Um, Miss Balogun?' he said.

'Yes?' she replied.

'All the books have gone. All that's left in the cupboard are the games.'

'What?' asked Miss Balogun, and went with Harrison to look for herself.

Sure enough, every shelf of the book cupboard was empty. Not only were there no geography textbooks, but all the other books had gone too! All that was left was a pile of board games, kept there for the last day of school.

'That's very odd,' said Miss Balogun. 'I'm sure they were here yesterday.' She frowned. First a disappearing swimming pool and now this. She felt like she needed a long lie down.

'It's a mystery,' said Harrison, trying hard not to smile or glance at his black hole, in case he gave himself away. Inside, of course, he was fizzing with delight! He didn't need to lose his temper ever again to get his own way! This was great!

'Excuse me, everyone,' said Miss Balogun, when they were back in the classroom. 'All our books seem to have . . . gone missing, so while I go to the office to try and track them down and to ask about Hector, I suggest you occupy yourselves with these.'

She held up the pile of board games and the children shrieked for joy!

That afternoon was one of the best of Harrison's life, right up there with his trip to the Science Museum and his visit to the safari park. By the time afternoon break arrived, all the children in his class were so grateful that Harrison had somehow managed to 'lose' all the school books and given them an afternoon off, that every single one of them gave him their biscuit as a thank you.

When he added his own extra biscuit for being Handy Helper, he nearly had an entire packet! He had to ask for an extra glass of milk so that he could finish them all off.

And what was even better was there was no Hector Broom to ruin it all by pushing him around or threatening him with his dastardly elastic band.

After school, as he walked home with his mother and Lana, it occurred to Harrison that he wouldn't have to put up with any of the things that made him cross or scared or worried ever again. Anything he didn't like could just disappear into the black hole. *Poof!* This was going to be brilliant!

He was so wrapped up in happy thoughts of making all the sprouts in the world disappear that he didn't notice he was dawdling way behind Lana and his mother, and when Mr Hardwick tapped him on the shoulder it took him a while to return to reality.

'I don't suppose you've seen her, have you,

Harrison?' Mr Hardwick asked. In his hand
was a leaflet with a photo of Blue on it. It
read:

LOST DOG

Please help us find our
beloved Blue!
We miss her so much.

Any information, please contact
Mr & Mrs Hardwick,
Farthings Cottage.

Reward promised.

'I'm going to put these on all the trees in
the lane, and all the lamp posts in the village,'
explained Mr Hardwick. 'Blue's out there

somewhere, I know she is.' Mr Hardwick's eyes were red, as if he had been crying, and Harrison suddenly felt very sorry for him.

He felt a pang of guilt. Blue had always seemed so terrifying to him; he hadn't really thought about how fond Mr and Mrs Hardwick must be of their dog. Perhaps he should tell Mr Hardwick the truth? After all, it wasn't like he had meant to send Blue into the nothingness of his black hole, it was an accident.

Harrison took a deep breath. It was time to tell Mr Hardwick what had really happend.

'Erm . . .' he said, trying to find the words. 'Mr Hardwick?'

'You've seen Blue!' exclaimed Mr Hardwick. 'Have you, Harrison? Have you?'

'Well . . . you see . . . she's in here,' said

Harrison, pointing at the black hole tied to his wrist.

'In your balloon?' Mr Hardwick asked, looking confused.

'It's not actually a balloon,' explained Harrison. 'It's a black hole. I was given it at a birthday party.'

Mr Hardwick looked even more confused and took a step towards the black hole to have a closer look.

'Don't touch it!' exclaimed Harrison. 'Or you'll get sucked inside.'

'Right,' said Mr Hardwick, in a way that made it very clear he hadn't the faintest idea what Harrison was talking about.

Harrison took another deep breath.

'Blue jumped inside when I wasn't looking,' he said. 'And she hasn't come back out.'

There was a long silence while Harrison waited for Mr Hardwick to get really cross and start shouting at him. Instead, Mr Hardwick's eyes filled with tears.

'Thank you, Harrison,' he said. 'I keep Blue right here, in my heart. But you . . .' He ruffled Harrison's hair. 'You can keep her in your balloon.'

'That's not really what I meant—' began Harrison.

'I'm sorry,' said Mr Hardwick. 'I meant to say: you can keep her in your black hole.'

And with that, he trudged off down the hill with his leaflets, leaving Harrison feeling very guilty indeed.

As Harrison walked up the path, he glanced over at the Hardwicks' front garden. Blue would usually be there, barking through the gaps in the fence. Was it true that once something fell into a black hole, it could never escape? Did that mean Blue was gone for ever?

Later that evening, Harrison felt even guiltier. Because while they were eating dinner (Lana gobbling her gammon and peas with gusto, while Harrison shoved his into his black hole), the phone rang.

'Really?' Harrison's father asked whoever was on the other end of the line. 'I'll certainly ask him. One moment.'

He put his hand over the mouthpiece.

'Harrison?'

Harrison looked up, wide-eyed. For a moment he thought he had been caught getting rid of his food.

'It's Hector Broom's mother. She says

Hector didn't come home from school. Everyone's out looking for him. Have you seen him?'

Harrison looked at his black hole, then back at his father.

'Well?' asked his father.

Harrison didn't want to lie, but he was too scared to tell the truth and, besides, when he'd tried to come clean earlier to Mr Hardwick, he hadn't believed him anyway. 'Not since lunchtime,' he said eventually. Which wasn't exactly a lie, but wasn't exactly the truth either.

He looked back at his now-empty plate. Having a black hole had been very useful and quite fun, but it turned out that disappearing things wasn't as simple as he'd thought . . .

Chapter Seven

That night, try as he might, Harrison simply couldn't sleep. And when he finally did, he had a terrible nightmare. He was by some roadworks when a black-and-white dog with Hector Broom's face appeared and jumped up at him. Harrison ducked, and the creature sailed right over his head and into a cement mixer. By the time they got the animal out, the cement had set, freezing its furry body mid-leap, with just Hector's face peeping out, and his mother had to feed him through a straw until a vet arrived with a chisel—

Harrison woke with a start. The black hole was tied to the end of his bed, just as it had been the night before, and now that it had digested a swimming pool, Hector Broom, an entire cupboard of school books and all of the food that Harrison hated, it was bigger than ever. As Harrison lay in bed, looking at it and thinking of poor Blue covered in cement, he had a Moment of Clarity. He knew what he had to do: he had to go to Shelley's grandmother's house, find Shelley and ask her how to get Blue and Hector back.

He got himself dressed double-quick,

untied the black hole and tiptoed out onto the landing. His parents' bedroom door was closed, so they must still be asleep. *That's a good thing*, he thought. If they saw him sneaking out this early, they might ask him some difficult questions.

Once downstairs, he found a pencil and a piece of paper and wrote:

Dear Mother and Father
I am going out for a walk for no reason.
I am absolutely not going to Shelley's grandmother's house.

Love, Harrison

Satisfied, Harrison folded the note and left it in the middle of the kitchen table where he could be sure his parents would see it. Going out on his own was against the rules, but if he was back before his parents woke up, they need never know. And, if they did wake up and found him gone, the note, he reasoned, would stop them worrying.

He pulled his jacket off the peg, squeezed his feet into his wellies, tied the black hole safely to his left wrist and stepped outside into the cold early-morning air.

The lane was empty and he saw, to his horror, that every tree was pasted with one of Mr Hardwick's leaflets. Wherever he looked, Blue's face stared back at him. Feeling guiltier than ever, he hurried down the hill to a little crooked house opposite the village school.

He unhitched the weather-beaten gate, crunched up the little gravel path to the purple front door, and lifted himself onto his tiptoes so that he could reach the brass door knocker.

There was no answer, so he knocked again. All the curtains were shut.

'Shelley!' he called through the letterbox, which he noticed was decorated with a snake swallowing its own tail. 'Shelley!' There was no answer. He was about to give up when one of the upper windows opened, and Shelley's grandmother popped her head through the curtains.

'*Sssshhhh!*' she said, in a voice that Harrison thought was quite loud for someone asking him to be quiet. 'Don't you know what time it is?'

'I can't "*sssshhh*",' said Harrison. 'I need to speak to Shelley.'

'She's not home.'

'Where is she?' asked Harrison.

Shelley's grandmother looked at one of her three wristwatches. 'Probably halfway across the Atlantic Ocean,' she said.

'It's an emergency,' said Harrison, holding up the black hole. 'Something terrible has happened!'

Shelley's grandmother frowned. 'You'd better come inside.'

It would be good for the sake of our story to say that seconds later the front door opened and Shelley's grandmother and Harrison continued their conversation, but sadly that wouldn't be entirely true. Instead, there was a Very Long Time When Nothing Much Happened At All. There was no sound from inside the house, and nothing for Harrison to do except wait. A postman strolled past with a sack of letters on a trolley, a woman walked down the street with her dog and the sun grew so hot that Harrison wished he hadn't worn his jacket.

He was beginning to wonder whether Shelley's grandmother had forgotten all about him, when he heard a clicking and whirring sound on the other side of the door. He peeked through the letterbox. Inside, he could just make out Shelley's grandmother's feet coming down the stairs on a very slow-moving stairlift. It felt wrong to watch someone when they couldn't see him, so Harrison closed the letterbox and waited patiently for the door to open.

It didn't. The postman worked his way up the other side of the street, the woman returned with her dog and Harrison took off his jacket. He took another peep through the letterbox. Shelley's grandmother's feet had made some progress, but they were still coming Very Slowly down the hall. Finally, just when Harrison was wondering whether he should come back after lunch, the door opened.

If Harrison had thought the letterbox on the door was strange, the inside of the house was even stranger. For a start, all the curtains were closed, and the only light was cast from old-fashioned oil lamps. And, from every direction, there came the sound of ticking. Harrison followed Shelley's grandmother down the hall to the sitting room and saw that every wall, shelf, table top and cubbyhole was home to some sort of clock: digital clocks, wind-up clocks, pendulum clocks, bedside clocks, carriage clocks, cuckoo clocks, alarm clocks, grandfather clocks and maritime clocks, all of them clicking and whirring impatiently.

'Sit,' said Shelley's grandmother, indicating a footstool.

'Thank you,' replied Harrison. 'Why do you have so many clocks?' he asked as he perched on the stool, keeping a careful hold of the black hole in case it accidentally swallowed something it shouldn't.

'Well, you see, I have a very important appointment and I don't want to miss it,' said Shelley's grandmother as she shuffled towards an armchair and sat down stiffly.

'What kind of appointment?' Harrison asked.

'An Appointment With Destiny,' said the old lady mysteriously. 'Now, you say there's a problem with your black hole?' she said, clearly wanting to change the subject.

'Yes,' said Harrison. 'Someone fell into it. And I need to know how to get them out.'

'Who, exactly?'

'Blue. She's my next-door neighbour's dog. And a boy called Hector Broom, from my school. So, I really need Shelley's help. When is she coming back?'

The clocks seemed to tick a little louder, as if to emphasise the long pause that followed.

'Maybe never,' said the old lady. 'She's

gone to South America. To the Very Large Telescope in Chile. It's on top of a mountain, where there are no clouds and the sky is the brightest and clearest on Earth. It's the best place in the world to be an astronomer. She's hoping they'll give her a job.'

'But how am I going to get Hector Broom and Blue out without Shelley?'

'There are three things you have to know about a black hole,' announced the old lady. 'Firstly, a black hole is black.'

'Right,' said Harrison, nodding. That one seemed quite obvious, if he was honest.

'Secondly, anything that touches it is pulled inside.'

'Yes,' said Harrison. He'd already seen that in action.

'And, thirdly,' continued the old lady,

'once something is inside it can never come out. Unless . . .'

'Unless what?' asked Harrison.

The old lady was quiet for a moment, as if she was deciding whether to trust Harrison with one of her deepest secrets.

'I think you had better come with me,' she said finally.

Harrison helped her to her feet. That part of their meeting took almost as long as everything else put together, but it's not directly relevant to our story, so I won't bore you with the detail. It wasn't pretty and included a very awkward moment where Harrison's head was used by the old lady as a sort of leaning post, and another one where she somehow ended up sitting on top of him on the floor. But, eventually, through luck, perseverance and brute strength, they found themselves out of the sitting room and back in the hallway, edging their way towards a large green door.

Chapter Eight

'This,' said Shelley's grandmother, 'is my life's work.'

The green door swung open and Harrison's eyes widened in excitement. This was not at all what he had been expecting. It was an enormous laboratory! The walls were crowded with glass pipes and flasks, in which strange mixtures bubbled and effervesced.

Giant metal stars hung from the ceiling, with sparks flying between them. And sitting right in the middle of it all was the most extraordinary-looking machine.

Its main component was a colossal brass ring, big enough to drive a car through. Surrounding the ring were twenty or so giant lasers, their bright blue beams focused on a single point at its centre, which was pulsing white. The lasers were surrounded by a tangle of wires, steel pipes and pumps, and the whole crazy contraption was sitting on an enormous circular platform, which was connected by a series of cogs and pulleys to an old bicycle.

Harrison looked at Shelley's grandmother in surprise.

'What does that do?' he asked.

'It makes black holes,' said Shelley's grandmother. 'Or, at least, I hope it does. I haven't quite perfected my technique.'

'I don't understand,' said Harrison. 'Shelley gave me this black hole, so she must know how to make them. Why don't you just ask her to show you?'

'Good question,' she said, smiling brightly. 'But, no, I'm afraid that wouldn't work. I need to discover them all by myself. Let's forget about the machine for a minute, while we go back to basics.' She pointed to a multicoloured globe which was sitting on one of the workbenches. 'Do you know what this is?'

Harrison nodded. 'It's Earth.'

'Exactly. Here's you and me, in England, and here —' she said, spinning the globe —

'across the Atlantic Ocean, is the Atacama Desert, where Shelley will shortly be. Now, we're all stuck to the Earth, aren't we?'

'Are we?' asked Harrison, checking the soles of his shoes.

'Yes,' said Shelley's grandmother. 'Because of gravity. People can jump a little bit off the ground, but they can't get off completely. But do you know what can?'

'Rockets?' Harrison suggested.

'Right. Rockets are powerful enough to fly from Earth. What else?'

Harrison shrugged. What else could escape from Earth except for rockets?

'I'll show you,' said Shelley's grandmother, as she searched for something under the bench. 'There's a switch here somewhere . . . Ah, there we go!'

The lights dimmed, and all the cities on the globe lit up.

'What do you see now?' she asked.

'Light?'

'Precisely. Light is the other thing that is able to escape the Earth. So, let me ask you another question.'

Harrison made his best Ready-to-Answer-Questions face.

'What would the Earth look like if light *couldn't* escape?'

'Ummm . . .' said Harrison.

'It would look like this,' said Shelley's grandmother, making her way slowly over to a second, scarier-looking globe, whose surface was completely black. 'A black hole.' She ran her hands over the smooth black surface. 'All its insides collapse into a teeny tiny dot. The bit you see is called the event horizon. And nothing that crosses that can *ever* come back. Unless . . .'

'Unless what?' asked Harrison, a hopeful feeling rising in his chest.

'Unless you use the black hole to travel in time.'

'*Riiiight,*' said Harrison, not really understanding and starting to think that maybe Shelley's grandmother was a little bit mad.

'I don't suppose you've heard of an Einstein-Rosen bridge?' asked the old lady.

Harrison shook his head. 'I've heard of Tower Bridge,' he tried. 'That's in London.'

'It is indeed,' said the old lady. 'Well, an Einstein-Rosen bridge is similar, except instead of taking you from one place to

'The edge is called the Event Horizon. And nothing that crosses that can ever come back.'

another, it takes you from one time to another. Some people call it a wormhole, but I don't much care for that phrase.'

'Sounds gross,' said Harrison. 'Like it would be full of slime.'

'Exactly,' said the old lady. 'Whereas an Einstein-Rosen bridge is truly a thing of beauty.'

'So how do you turn a black hole into a Heinz-Frozen bridge?' asked Harrison.

'Einstein-Rosen. And that's just the problem,' said the old lady, her eyes gleaming in the darkness. 'I have absolutely no idea.'

That night, as Harrison lay in bed trying to fall asleep, he came to a decision. The black hole had to go. Despite looking really cool and being a great place to hide overcooked vegetables, it was almost certainly what grown-ups would call a health-and-safety nightmare. And while it had been fun, it was all getting a bit too serious now.

No, it was time to get rid of it. So, once he was sure everyone in the house was asleep, he put on his dressing gown and slippers, untied the black hole from the bottom of his bed and tiptoed downstairs. With a bit of luck, he reasoned, his black hole would look like a discarded party balloon and it would be taken away with the rubbish.

Outside, the sky was in chaos. High clouds drifted slowly across a full moon, while low clouds scurried towards the horizon in completely the opposite direction. A storm was coming in, and the leaves of the mulberry tree shimmered restlessly. Harrison made his way stealthily and silently to the Bin Palace, which was what his father called the shed-without-a-roof at the end of the front garden, where all the bins were kept. A shaft of moonlight hit the ground and cast a sharp shadow of Harrison and his black hole on the lawn. After double-checking that no one was watching, he tied the black hole to the handle of the large black bin. The green one, he was fairly sure, was for garden waste only.

He checked the lane once more to make extra-triple-sure no one had seen him, then he shut the door of the Bin Palace, pulled his dressing gown tightly round him and scuttled back into the house.

No sooner had the front door closed, the

wind picked up and the bins began to rattle. A tissue blew out of one of the recycling boxes and scurried up into the night sky, like an angel being called back to heaven. A blue plastic sack full of cardboard jostled a large white canvas bag, spewing plastic milk bottles onto the pavement. The lid of the large green bin flipped open and grass clippings took to the wind like confetti. Finally, the black bin shuddered, as if it was catching a summer chill, and the black hole caught the wind, its string pulling tight. And, slowly, the knot that Harrison had tied began to unravel . . .

Chapter Nine

To Harrison's great relief, the next morning everything felt like it was back to normal. He'd had a restful sleep, free of anxious dreams about Hector Broom and Blue. And there was no black hole tied to the bottom of his bed.

But when he arrived in the kitchen ready for his breakfast, there was no sign of his parents or sister, which was most definitely *not* normal.

Maybe they've slept in, he thought.

He climbed the stairs to check their bedrooms. He looked in on Lana, who was still fast asleep. But his parents' bed was empty. Where were they?

He went downstairs again and this time he noticed the front door was ever so slightly ajar. He put on his shoes and went to investigate.

With a sigh of relief, he saw his mother and father standing in the front garden, looking over the fence. And they weren't alone. All their neighbours from the lane were there too, chattering excitedly and pointing at something just out of sight.

Harrison walked over to see what was going on and when he reached the grown-ups, he could hardly believe his eyes.

The Hardwicks' cottage had completely disappeared!

All of it. The walls, the roof, the windows . . . all gone! The only thing that remained was the floor: the grey-and-white squares of lino from the kitchen, the mustard-coloured carpets from the front room and the balding doormat that had been just inside the back door. The only piece of furniture left was the downstairs loo, bolted to the floor in the middle of a square of faded pink carpet. And there, hovering right in the middle of it all, was the black hole, now twice the size it had been the night before.

Harrison gulped.

'I've heard of a roof blowing off,' Chris the farmer was saying, 'and maybe the odd window being broken in a storm. But never anything like this.'

'Those walls were made of solid stone,' said Jinnie from Cuckoo Cottage. 'There's not a wind in the world could shift that.'

'Isn't that your balloon, Harrison?' asked his father. 'What's that doing there?'

'Umm . . . ' said Harrison, not really sure how he could explain everything to his father. This was like something from a nightmare. Somehow, his black hole must have got loose in the wind and swallowed the cottage, with the Hardwicks inside it! He had to get it back, or it might gobble up the entire street!

'Maybe . . .' began Harrison's mother.

Everyone turned to look at her.

'Maybe they moved it. The house. In the night.'

'Moved it?' asked Chris.

'Yes,' said Harrison's mother, not sounding sure at all. 'Stone by stone. I've heard of people doing that, if they really love a house and they have enough money. Maybe the Hardwicks are eccentric millionaires and we just never knew it.'

Everyone fell silent. Eccentric millionaires moving an entire cottage seemed extremely unlikely, but no one else could think of another explanation that made more sense.

Harrison quietly started to walk down the garden path, towards the garden gate.

'The really strange thing is that there's no debris anywhere else,' Chris said. 'Not a chip of stone, not a scrap of wood, not a flake of slate. It's like the cottage vanished into thin air.'

Which was when Harrison heard his father say: 'Harrison? What do you think you're doing?'

Harrison, who was now halfway up the Hardwicks' garden path, stopped in his tracks.

'Nothing,' replied Harrison.

'Don't say "nothing",' said his father. 'You're obviously doing something.'

'I'm fetching my balloon,' said Harrison, trying to look innocent.

The wind was picking up again and the black hole started to drift.

'You're just going to have to leave it there,' his father told him. 'Someone's kidnapped the Hardwicks and stolen their house. It's too dangerous for you to be wandering around, and the police are going to have to dust for fingerprints. We must leave everything untouched.'

'But I need it,' argued Harrison.

'Don't be silly,' said his father. 'No one *needs* a balloon. People need cars and knee operations and slotted spoons to drain pasta. Nobody *needs* a balloon.'

Harrison had to think quickly. 'I'm taking it to Show and Tell,' he said, crossing his fingers behind his back once again.

'Show and Tell?' his mother asked. 'I thought that was just in Reception?'

'It's a special one for the whole school,' Harrison fibbed.

Out of the corner of his eye, he saw that the black hole had moved across the Hardwicks' garden towards the fence. He needed to grab its string before it did any more damage!

Thankfully, at that very moment, a fire engine came clanking up the lane and hissed to a halt outside the Hardwicks' cottage. Or rather, it hissed to a halt outside where the Hardwicks' cottage used to be. Two red-faced fire fighters clambered down from the cab, and all the grown-ups rushed to tell them what had happened. Harrison seized his chance and raced after the black hole as fast as his legs would carry him, but just as his hand was closing around the string, there was a downward gust of wind and the black hole rushed upwards!

Harrison watched in horror as it leapt the fence and took flight. It was heading straight for his sister's bedroom!

Without a moment's delay, Harrison raced across the front garden, in through the open front door and up the stairs. He grabbed the footstool from the bathroom, sprinted to his sister's room and placed it under the open skylight. Through the open window, Harrison could see the string of the black hole, twitching as if it was alive.

He tried to reach the black hole, though even with the stool he was just too short to grab the string. Thinking quickly, he jumped down, grabbed all of Lana's storybooks and stacked them on the top step of the footstool. He climbed back on top of them, which brought him a little closer, but the string was still way out of reach.

'*Aargh!*' he cried in frustration.

Lana, who up until that point had been sleeping peacefully, despite the kerfuffle, stirred and rubbed her eyes. 'What you doin'?' she asked, sitting up in bed.

'Trying to stop us being eaten alive!' said Harrison.

'Do you want to play cleaning?' asked Lana, not grasping the seriousness of the situation at all. 'Cleaning' was her favourite game. She had a little toy cleaning cart with a bucket and mop, a feather duster and her very own toy squeegee mop.

'Not now! We're about to be disappeared!' replied Harrison, running to his bedroom. 'Where is it? Where is it?' he asked, as he flung toy after toy out from under his bed.

'Ah ha!' he exclaimed, holding up his Robot Claw in triumph.

He ran back into Lana's room and climbed on the stool again. All he needed to do now was grab the string with the Claw. But it wasn't at all easy. The black hole was bobbing and weaving in the wind, its string fluttering behind it like the tail of a kite.

'Do you want to clean the window?' asked Lana, offering Harrison the bucket in a way that wasn't very helpful at all.

'Lana!' called Harrison, looking down at her in frustration. Suddenly the Claw lurched in his hand, as if gripped by an extremely powerful force. Glancing back up, Harrison saw that the tips of its fingers were touching the black hole!

'Lana! Help!' called Harrison, feeling that not only was he about to lose his Robot Claw, but himself as well. He thought Lana might see the danger he was in and hang onto his legs, but instead she tickled his right knee with her toy feather duster.

'It's pulling me in!' he cried.

Lana turned her attention to his left knee.

His feet began to leave the footstool!

Harrison stared at the black hole. It was like looking into some sort of tunnel, while time and space swirled around him. Was that Blue he could see, somersaulting round and round? And the Hardwicks' cottage, rolling and tumbling like a jumper in a tumble drier? Harrison was gripped by a terrible curiosity: what would happen if he didn't let go? What would it be like inside a one hundred per cent genuine black hole?

He looked at his knuckles, turning white as he gripped the handle of the Robot Claw . . .

And let go.

For a few awesome seconds, he seemed to

'Lana! Help!' called Harrison, feeling that not only was he about
to lose his Robot Claw, but himself as well.

balance in mid-air, as if the black hole was deciding whether to swallow him or spit him out . . .

And then he fell with a clatter onto the floor.

Very helpfully, Lana put the cleaning bucket on his head.

'I'm hungry,' she said. 'I want some toast.'

Harrison pulled the bucket off his head and watched the black hole through the open skylight. Frozen on its surface was the Robot Claw, slowly fading from view. That had been a Very Close Call Indeed. And what was he going to do now? He couldn't just leave the black hole hovering outside.

Harrison's eyes came to rest on Lana's squeegee mop.

That might work. He could use the mop to

grab the string!

Getting back up on the footstool, he raised the mop up through the skylight, worked the handle and watched the sponge close on the string of the black hole.

As gently as he could, Harrison pulled the black hole in through the open skylight, taking care that it didn't touch the window frame. Then he drew the head of the squeegee mop towards him, hand over hand, until he could get a firm grasp on the string.

Harrison breathed a huge sigh of relief.

Then his stomach sank again as he realised what he had to do. It was time to tell his parents the truth.

Chapter Ten

'Hector Broom is where?' asked Harrison's father.

'In here,' said Harrison, pointing to his black hole.

'Hector Broom is in your balloon?'

'It's not a balloon,' said Harrison, for what felt like the hundredth time. 'It's a black hole.'

Telling the truth was turning out to be quite difficult, as neither his mother nor father seemed to be able to understand what he was trying to say.

Harrison's mother and father looked at one another.

'Harrison, it's not helpful for you to tell us lies when Hector is missing,' said Harrison's mother.

'I'm not lying!' said Harrison, starting to feel frustrated. 'He's in there. So is Blue. And all our school books, some broccoli, and Elmond the elephant.'

'Who's Elmond the elephant?' asked Harrison's father, looking more bewildered than ever.

'*Tshh*,' tutted Harrison's mother. 'One of Harrison's soft toys.'

'Ah, yes,' said Harrison's father, as if he had known that all along, which he hadn't.

'Is there anything else in your "black hole"?' asked his mother.

'Well, let's see. The gammon from last night, my school dinner from yesterday, the bike shed and the shallow swimming pool.'

There was a long pause while nothing much happened. His mother's mouth opened and closed a few times, but no words came out. Then his father smiled. And then he started to giggle.

'Sorry,' he said, trying to keep a straight face. 'I thought for a moment there you said the bike shed and a swimming pool.'

'I did,' said Harrison.

'Don't be silly,' said his mother, with a chuckle.

'I'm not being silly!' said Harrison. 'Throw something in and you'll see!'

'You can't just own a black hole,' said his father.

'You can!' exclaimed Harrison. 'And I do!'

'Now, really—' Harrison's mother began.

'*Euuurrgghhhhh!*' groaned Harrison.

'Uh-oh,' said Harrison's father, backing away. 'Code Red.'

'*AAAAAARRRRRRGGGGGGHHHHH!*' bellowed Harrison. 'I HATE IT SO MUCH WHEN YOU SAY THAT!'

And before he knew what he was doing, Harrison began to swing his black hole around him, faster and faster.

'Harrison! Calm down!' called his father.

'And tell the truth!' cried his mother.

'*EEUUURRRGH!*' wailed Harrison.

Round and round Harrison spun, so that eventually all he could see was the black hole, while the rest of the world became a blur behind it.

'WHY WON'T ANYONE BELIEVE ME??!!' he screamed.

But no one replied.

Harrison began to feel dizzy. Then he began to feel sick. Then he stopped spinning.

The kitchen wobbled back into focus. There was Lana, sitting at the kitchen table, colouring her unicorn's tail with a purple crayon. There was her egg, simmering on the stove. And there was his black hole, swaying above his head. In other words, everything was exactly as it had been before.

Except . . .

There was no sign of his parents.

Whatsoever.

'I'm hungry,' said Lana, looking up from her drawing.

Once, when Harrison had got really cross in a department store because he had been told he couldn't have a toy he wanted, instead of telling him off, or trying to get him to calm down, his parents had hidden in a rack of coats. *Maybe they are hiding now*, thought Harrison.

But when he looked, his parents weren't in any of the cupboards or under the table, or indeed anywhere else in the kitchen that it was possible to hide. A Troublesome Thought lodged itself in his brain and he tried his hardest to ignore it.

'Where's Daddy?' asked Lana.

'Nowhere,' Harrison told her. 'I mean . . .

somewhere but maybe not here.'

'Where's Mummy?'

'Yes,' Harrison replied. It wasn't much of an answer, but with his mind whirring, it was all he could manage. Was it possible that in his rage he had swept their parents up in his black hole?

'Eggy eggy!' shouted Lana.

'Okay,' said Harrison, having another Troublesome Thought. If their mother and father were in the black hole, did that mean he was now in charge?

'Eggy eggy!' Lana repeated.

'What's the magic word?' asked Harrison.

'Eggy eggy!' shouted Lana, twice as loudly.

'Please,' corrected Harrison. And as he said it, he suddenly realised why his parents were always saying the same to him. After all, it really isn't very nice when someone orders you about without being polite.

'*Pleeease*,' said Lana, in the same tone of voice that you might say, 'Oh, stop bothering me.'

Harrison decided the only way he could get her to be quiet, so he could come up with a plan, would be to give her some food. But feeding a three-year-old turned out to be a lot harder than it looked. No sooner had Harrison managed to serve Lana her egg than she wanted the top cutting off. No sooner had he blown on it to get it to the perfect temperature than she demanded salt on top. No sooner had he found her a cushion to get her to exactly the right height than she wanted a glass of water. By the time breakfast was over, Harrison was completely exhausted.

Was this what his parents went through every day? No wonder they were always complaining.

Suddenly, he found himself missing them really badly. What would he do without them?

If his father wasn't there, who would give him a slice of toast and peanut butter if he woke up feeling hungry? And without his mother, who would tuck him into bed at night and read him a story?

Was he going to spend the rest of his life without seeing them ever again?

He felt his throat tighten and his eyes prick with tears.

'Don't cry, Haddy,' said Lana.

He quickly wiped his eyes so she wouldn't

see him crying. If his sister found out that their mother and father were stuck in a black hole, she would be really upset.

No. He had to get his parents back. Whatever it took.

Chapter Eleven

Which is why, half an hour later, Harrison found himself pushing Lana's toy ambulance up the gravel path to Shelley's grandmother's purple front door, with Lana at the steering wheel and his black hole tied to the roof.

I don't know if you've ever tried pushing a toy ambulance up a gravel path, but if you have, you'll know it's very noisy. In Harrison's case, it was so noisy that he completely failed to hear the extraordinary sound that was coming from inside the cottage until he was right outside its front door.

He pushed open the letterbox and peered through.

Inside, every clock was ringing: digital clocks, wind-up clocks, pendulum clocks, bedside clocks, carriage clocks, cuckoo clocks, alarm clocks, grandfather clocks and maritime clocks, each of them straining to make their own voice heard. It was deafening. And there, at the other end of the hall, was Shelley's grandmother, shuffling slowly back and forth, muttering to herself.

'Hello!' called Harrison.

'Hello!' called Lana in reply.

'I'm talking to Shelley's grandmother,' explained Harrison.

'I'm hungry,' replied Lana. 'I want a biscuit.'

Harrison pushed his right arm through the letterbox and waved. 'Shelley's grandmother. It's me, Harrison!' he shouted. But it was no use. The clocks were ringing so loudly there was no way the old lady could hear him.

Harrison felt something prickling the inside of his elbow. It seemed to be a piece of string with one end attached to the inside of the door; the other end felt loose. He gave it a pull, and out it came, with a door key attached to the end of it!

For a moment, Harrison hesitated. He didn't want to give Shelley's grandmother a fright by breaking into her house. Then he remembered that if he didn't get his parents out of the black hole, he and Lana might never see them again, and he decided it was worth the risk. So he untied his black hole from the roof of the ambulance and slotted the key into the lock on the front door. It fitted perfectly, and the next thing he knew, he and Lana were standing in the hallway.

He needn't have worried about scaring Shelley's grandmother. She was so deep in thought that she behaved as if having two small children sneak into her house uninvited was the most natural thing in the world. Harrison had to stand right in her path, waving both arms, before she even acknowledged their presence.

'I need to find Shelley!' he called, trying to make himself heard over the din of the clocks.

'What?' replied Shelley's grandmother, cupping her hand to her ear. 'I can't hear you.'

'I said . . .' began Harrison, and then paused. The alarm nearest him, an old-fashioned bedside clock with two bells, suddenlystoppedringing. Thenthemechanical cuckoo in the clock above him closed its beak, fell silent and sprang back behind closed doors. Then, in twos and threes, and dozens and scores, all the other clocks fell silent too, until the only sound remaining was the bleep of Shelley's grandmother's digital watch.

For a moment, they all stood staring at it, until Harrison stepped forward and switched it off.

'Thank you,' said Shelley's grandmother. 'I've never been able to work that thing.'

'I need to find Shelley!' exclaimed Harrison one more time, but Shelley's grandmother put her finger to her lips, signalling for him to be silent.

'Out of the question,' she said.

'I want a biscuit,' said Lana. 'A pink wafer.'

'Have you any idea,' asked Shelley's grandmother, shaking her head in disbelief, 'what's happening here?'

'No,' said Harrison, because he didn't.

'It's time,' announced Shelley's grandmother. 'For my Appointment With Destiny!'

She pushed on the green door, and about ten minutes later, after a considerable amount of huffing and puffing and having a little break to catch their breath, they found themselves in her laboratory.

Only this time, instead of a pulsing white light, at the centre of the machine was an enormous black disc.

'You made a black hole!' exclaimed Harrison.

'Three, actually,' said Shelley's grandmother, puffing herself up with pride. 'I made the first just before breakfast. Unfortunately, it wasn't stable. After breakfast, I made the second. But it wasn't big enough for me to climb into. Then I made this! Then I had to stop because of my crossing duty, which, by the way, I noticed you two weren't there for.'

'Sorry about that,' said Harrison.

'Not a problem,' said Shelley's grandmother.

'It's a busy time. The point is, I've made a black hole and now I need to turn it into an Einstein-Rosen bridge. Only I've still got no idea how!'

'But-but . . . where are you going?' asked Harrison.

'The future!' cried the old lady. 'To a time where anyone can do anything, and that includes young girls who want to be astronomers!'

'But you can't leave! I need you to help me get my parents back,' said Harrison. 'I got really cross and then spun around, like this!' He demonstrated with his black hole, being careful not to touch Lana or Shelley's grandmother – he didn't need anyone else falling in! 'And then they got sucked inside! I have to get them out!'

'Chocolate finger?' said Lana.

'Impossible!' said Shelley's grandmother.

'Please!' begged Harrison.

'Or an Oreo?' said Lana, with even more feeling.

Shelley's grandmother turned to an enormous blackboard that was covered in complicated-looking maths. 'I don't have time to help you! I've only got seven minutes left! And I still haven't figured out how to turn this into an Einstein-Rosen bridge!'

She rubbed her chin furiously, as if she was trying to figure out the answer to a very difficult problem. Then her eye caught a biscuit tin which was standing among some tea things on a workbench.

'Here's a Garibaldi,' she said to Lana.

'But what am I supposed to do?' yelled

Harrison.

'Wait!' exclaimed Shelley's grandmother. 'Did you say you *spun* round?'

'What?' asked Harrison.

'When your parents fell into the hole, you said you were spinning?'

Harrison nodded.

'Of course!' exclaimed Shelley's grandmother, with a triumphant look in her eye. 'That's it! The black hole should be spinning . . .'

She scribbled some elaborate maths on the board.

'Yes!' she cried. 'A spinning black hole forms an Einstein-Rosen bridge.' She checked one of her three watches. 'There's still time!' she said to Harrison. 'Quick! I need you to pedal as fast as you can!'

'No!' said Harrison. 'You have to help me!' He couldn't possibly rescue his parents or Blue, or even Hector Broom, unless he found Shelley, but the old lady wasn't listening to him! What was wrong with all these grown-ups? His heart began to race as anger boiled up inside! He wanted so badly to kick and yell and tell Shelley's grandmother exactly what he thought of her, but . . .

He didn't.

Instead, he took a deep breath. And another deep breath. And another.

And then, in the calmest voice he could muster, he said: 'Not until you tell me where Shelley is. I'm really scared that without her I'll never see my parents again.'

'Fine,' said Shelley's grandmother, with a roll of her eyes, and handed Harrison a postcard. On it was a picture of a telescope, perched high on a mountain. 'Shelley's here.'

Harrison took the postcard with a sigh of relief. It had worked. Being calm and asking simply for help rather than yelling and screaming meant that he now knew where to find Shelley.

'Now, can we please do this? I'm running out of time!' Shelley's grandmother said with a tut. Without so much as another word, she took Harrison's black hole and tied it safely out of Lana's reach, then hoisted him onto the seat of the bicycle. Harrison could only just touch the pedals, but by standing up off the seat, and leaning all his weight forward, he managed to get them moving.

A giant pulley began to turn and the whole machine revolved, like a colossal version of

Shelley's grandmother's black globe.

'Faster!' yelled Shelley's grandmother, pointing at a dial. 'Faster!'

Harrison pedalled as fast as he could.

'Good,' said Shelley's grandmother. 'Now keep it steady while I check something . . .'

She scribbled a few more calculations on the board.

'Right. I need to hit that thing at forty-two miles an hour! Wish me luck!'

Harrison was expecting her to run and jump into the black hole. But he'd forgotten, of course, that the old lady didn't move with that much speed. Instead, he watched as she clambered slowly onto a mobility scooter and released the brake.

The next few moments were a bit boring, as nothing much happened. Harrison kept on pedalling, Lana nibbled on her biscuit and Shelley's grandmother trundled slowly towards her spinning black hole.

Harrison was just beginning to wonder how much longer he could keep up the pace with his pedalling, when the front tyre of the mobility scooter touched the edge of the black hole, and the old lady shot into the void with uncharacteristic speed, until all Harrison could see were the

rear tyres, frozen in time. Soon even they had faded from view, and Shelley's grandmother was gone.

'I don't like Gary Baldy,' said Lana, and threw her half-eaten Garibaldi biscuit into the middle of the black hole.

Harrison stopped pedalling. What was he going to do now?

Chapter Twelve

For a few moments after Shelley's grandmother disappeared, Harrison felt very lost and alone.

His parents had vanished into his black hole and now the only grown-up other than Shelley who could have helped him was gone too.

As he climbed down from the bicycle seat,

his eyes began to tingle with tears for the second time that day.

'Gone,' said Lana, pointing at the giant black hole.

'Yes,' Harrison replied.

Lana looked worried.

'Don't worry, Lana,' he said, with more confidence than he felt. 'It's all going to be all right.'

He looked down at the postcard Shelley's grandmother had given him. He turned it over and read what was on the back:

Dear Shelley,
Don't forget your Appointment
With Destiny!

9.09 a.m. 9 September 2019

Yours, Shelley

The Crooked House

Hilcot

Nr. Sheepston

UK

He frowned. Why was it from Shelley to Shelley? Did Shelley and her grandmother have the same name? That was odd.

Harrison turned the postcard over again, so that he could look at the picture. In very small writing, in one corner, it said:

Very Large Telescope, Mount Paranal, Chile.

Harrison took a deep breath. He was eight years old. How was he ever going to get to Chile? And who would look after Lana while he was gone? It was impossible.

Which was when he remembered the one person who could help him.

When Harrison opened the front door of the cottage the following morning, he hardly recognised the teenager standing on the step. He was wearing mirror shades and a faded green army jacket, and his hair was gelled in a quiff.

'Greetings, H,' the boy said. 'I came as soon as I could.'

'Sonny!' Harrison rushed forward and gave his big brother a hug. In fact, Sonny was actually Harrison's half-brother because they had the same father, though Sonny lived with his mother in London.

Harrison had phoned Sonny last night and told him everything that had happened. Sonny might not be a grown-up, but now that his brother was here, Harrison was sure he could help him fix everything.

'Where's Lana?' asked Sonny, removing his shades.

'At school,' said Harrison proudly. 'I gave her breakfast too.'

'That's really impressive,' said Sonny, following his brother through to the kitchen. 'Wait . . . what happened here?'

The entire kitchen was empty. All that was left was the black hole, tied to the back of the last remaining chair. The table, the pots, the pans, the crockery, the cutlery, the coffee maker, the fridge, all of them were gone.

'I have to keep feeding it,' explained Harrison, 'or it will shrink to nothing.'

'I see,' said Sonny gravely. 'And that's where Dad and your mum are?' he asked, waving his hand near the black hole's surface to see if he could see any reflection.

'It was an accident,' said Harrison. 'And I would say sorry, except I can't, because they're in there and I'm out here. That's why I have to keep throwing things in, because I don't know what will happen if it vanishes completely.'

'Hmmm . . .' said Sonny. 'You said on the phone that you need to go to Chile to find this Shelley person. But how are you going to get the black hole on a plane? You can't check it in; the plane would disappear. Guess you'll have to take it as hand luggage.'

'A plane?' asked Harrison.

'How else are you going to get to Chile?' replied Sonny.

'But do they let children fly on their own?' asked Harrison.

'Never,' said Sonny. 'But they let teenagers.'

'Where are you travelling to, sir?' asked the lady at the check-in, glancing up at the tall, raincoat-wearing gentleman in mirror shades.

'Santiago,' said Harrison. He had the string of his black hole in his left hand, so with his right hand, he reached into his inside pocket and handed over Sonny's passport. As the sleeves on his father's raincoat were much too long, he had bunched them up under his armpits so no one would notice.

The lady tapped away at her keyboard, then frowned at her screen.

'And how old are you?' she asked.

'Thirteen,' replied Harrison, not daring to catch her eye. 'My parents gave me this letter,' he said, handing over an envelope. Of course his parents had done nothing of the sort; Sonny had written it on the computer and forged their father's signature.

The lady frowned, then tapped on the keyboard again and frowned some more. She picked up Sonny's passport and studied it very carefully. She looked up at Harrison.

'Would you mind taking your sunglasses off?' she asked.

'Of course,' said Harrison, hoping she would fall for his disguise.

He and Sonny looked alike, but not that alike. That morning, on their way to the train station, they had asked the taxi to stop off at a hairdresser called Hairs R Us.

'My little brother really wants to look like me,' Sonny had said to Karl ('with a K'), the man in charge, pretending to be embarrassed.

'I'm not that little,' said Harrison.

'So we're going to give you a quiff, then, are we?' asked Karl.

'And I want it to be brown too,' said Harrison, whose hair was blond. He caught Sonny's eye and his brother winked.

'Really?' asked Karl. 'Do your parents know about this?'

'Yeah, they said it was totally fine,' said Sonny, in his most teenage of teenage voices. 'They've given us cash,' he said, flashing a couple of twenty pound notes.

'In that case,' said Karl. 'You can have it purple with pink spots.'

Now, as he stood at the check-in desk, Harrison just hoped that the haircut and dye would be enough to convince the lady that he was his older brother.

The lady continued to stare at the screen.

And then . . . 'Do you have any luggage to check in?' she asked.

Harrison blinked. Did this mean she was going to let him on the plane?

'No,' he said.

'Any hand luggage?'

Harrison looked at the black hole.

'Just this,' he said.

There was a long pause, while the lady studied something on her screen.

'You'll be boarding from Gate C52,' she said, and handed Harrison the passport. Inside it was a freshly-printed boarding pass. 'Have a good flight.'

Harrison thanked her, put the sunglasses back on, turned and walked straight into one of the shiny metal posts that told you where to queue. The problem, of course, was that he was sitting on Sonny's shoulders, and Sonny couldn't properly see where he was going.

'Sorry, everyone,' said Harrison to the annoyed-looking people in the queue. 'Careful!' he hissed down at his brother. 'We don't want to get caught out. Come on, let's find the loo and get out of this coat.'

He spotted a woman pushing an elderly gentleman in a special airport wheelchair. She was wearing a badge that said: *Chris Difford, Special Assistance.* 'Excuse me,' he said to her. 'Where's the loo?'

'That way,' the woman said, pointing down a busy corridor to their left.

'Thank you,' said Harrison. And they began to head slowly away, trying their best not to bash into anything else.

As soon as they were safely inside a cubicle in the loo with the door locked, Harrison tied his black hole to the loo seat, and began to unbutton the raincoat. When he got to the third button, Sonny's hair appeared, and by the time he reached the fifth, he could see his brother's red and sweaty face.

'We made it!' hissed Harrison, in great excitement. 'I've got my boarding pass, look. Now I can get on the plane.'

'Not quite,' replied Sonny. 'We need to get you and your black hole through the security scanner first and I'm not sure how it's going to cope with that. What if they want to take it from you to examine it?'

Harrison's heart began to race. If the scanner people took his black hole, he'd never get his parents back! He suddenly felt

Very Scared Indeed. And because he was scared, he started to have a meltdown.

'I don't want to go on a plane!' he blurted.

'*Sssh!*' whispered Sonny. 'Someone will hear!'

'It's a stupid idea! You can't make me!' yelled Harrison. His legs wobbled and his arms flailed, as if they had minds of their own.

'Get a grip!' said Sonny, clamping his hand over Harrison's mouth. 'If you pull a Code Red, we're finished!'

A Code Red! Now Sonny was using that horrible phrase his parents did! Urgh!

But, suddenly, Harrison had a revolutionary thought. What if he didn't lose his temper? Just like with Shelley's grandmother back at the lab, when he'd managed to make her listen to him. What if, instead of kicking off, he imagined putting his problem in the black hole and . . . making it disappear? What if he just told Sonny that he was worried, not angry?

And, for just a moment, he relaxed.

'What's the matter?' asked Sonny. 'Are you all right?' He still had his hand over Harrison's mouth.

Harrison tried to speak, but it came out muffled.

'Sorry,' whispered Sonny, and released his hand.

'I'm scared,' said Harrison in a small voice.

'That's okay,' said Sonny with a smile. 'So am I. But we are not going to let this thing beat us. We're going to think, and we're going to come up with a plan.'

There was a pause, while the two of them did just that . . .

Harrison considered various options, including squirting all the security people with a water pistol so that they ran away, or setting off the fire alarm, like Hector Broom had once done at school. Unfortunately, he didn't have a water pistol and he had no idea if airports had fire alarms. He was just considering a third option that he liked to call 'Giving Up', when his eye caught a notice on the door in front of them. It said that the toilet they were in was 'Accessible' and showed a little stick man sign of a disabled person.

'What if I was in a wheelchair?' Harrison asked. 'Like the old man we just saw. What would they do at security then?"

'I think they'd wave you straight through,' said Sonny. 'But you're not in a wheelchair, so that's no good . . .'

'What if I pretended?' whispered Harrison, a note of excitement in his voice. 'I look really tall sitting on your shoulders. What if I say I've had a growth spurt, and it's given me really bad growing pains?'

'Harrison,' said Sonny, with the air of someone breaking bad news. 'Impersonating a disabled person is wrong. And no one, I repeat, no one, is going to give you special assistance because you've got growing pains.'

'Bring him straight through, Chris.'

The security guard was beckoning, so

Chris Difford from Special Assistance pushed Harrison/Sonny's wheelchair through a tall grey rectangular arch, which Harrison guessed must be some sort of metal detector. It was like being invisible. No one searched him, and no one questioned the fact that he was holding what looked like a large black party balloon on a piece of string.

That wasn't even the best bit. Once they were through security, Chris helped Harrison onto a special silver-and-yellow mini-truck and drove through the airport like a maniac, all the way to the boarding gate. Then she helped Harrison/Sonny back into the wheelchair, and pushed him down a long winding corridor, right to the door of the plane.

'Here you go, my friend,' said Chris,

parking the wheelchair and ratcheting the brake with her foot. 'End of the line.'

'Thanks,' said Harrison. There was a porthole in the wall, and he could see a huge jet engine spinning on the wing of the plane.

There were two flight attendants waiting inside, a man and a woman. They both smiled brightly.

'Look after this one, please' Chris told them. 'Teenager. Growing pains.'

'Right,' said the lady flight attendant, slightly mystified. 'Welcome on board, sir. May I see your boarding pass?'

Harrison handed it over, and she studied it carefully, as if she was looking for some sort of mistake. Then she smiled.

'You're at the back,' she said. 'Row twenty-six.'

As soon as Harrison reached his seat, Sonny started poking him in the ribs. Harrison checked to see if the flight attendants were looking, then undid the top few buttons of his coat.

'Unbelievable,' said Sonny, peeping through the gap. 'We made it.'

'What do we do now?' asked Harrison. It felt very strange talking to his chest.

'Somehow, I need to get off this plane,' Sonny replied. 'I've got to get back so I can look after Lana when school's finished. Otherwise she'll be all on her own, or worse, someone will find out that Dad and your mum are gone.'

The first few passengers were making their way down the plane towards them, so they needed to move fast. Making sure his black hole was securely tied to the armrest of the seat next to him, Harrison unbuttoned his coat and carefully climbed off his brother's shoulders.

Sonny was now looking very red in the face and his quiff was squashed.

'Right, little brother,' he said, standing up and putting his hand on Harrison's shoulders. 'You're on your own from here. Good luck!'

And then he was gone.

Chapter Thirteen

'**Y**ou sure you got the money for this, kid?'

The taxi driver turned off the highway, and the road began to wind upwards into the Atacama Desert.

'Absolutely,' said Harrison. 'My brother gave me a whole load of dollars. Like, two hundred. And you said this would cost sixty.

So I've got plenty.'

'Did I say sixty?' said the taxi driver. 'I mean seventy. Or maybe eighty. It's hard to tell. Depends on the meter.'

'But your meter isn't on,' Harrison pointed out.

'I know,' replied the taxi driver. 'That's why it's hard to tell.'

Harrison gave his black hole a nervous glance. It was tied to the door handle, and if he put his head out of the open window and peered upwards, he could see it leaning into the wind, way above him. The problem was, it was shrinking rapidly. After two plane journeys, with nothing to eat but an in-flight magazine and some of Harrison's plane food, it had dwindled to the size of a grapefruit.

As soon as he got to the telescope, he would

have to feed it, but for now, all he could do was watch the desert glide by.

Harrison had never been to Mars, but if he ever got the chance to go, he imagined it would look a lot like the view that was unfolding outside his window. Everywhere he looked was red. Red dust lay in drifts by the side of the road, red boulders roasted in the sunshine and red mountains pierced the bright blue sky.

And what made it even more like Mars was that there seemed to be no sign of life. That morning, he had flown over lush green fields to land at Santiago Airport, and as he'd climbed down the steps of the plane, the air had felt hot and damp, like the inside of a greenhouse. From there, after claiming to be very small for his age, he had got on a much smaller plane and flown to a much drier, dustier place called Antofagasta. As the taxi left the airport, Harrison had seen a row of wilting palm trees, lining the highway. But the Atacama was so desolate, it made Antofagasta look like a tropical oasis.

'Are there any animals up here?' asked Harrison.

'Nn-nh,' replied the taxi driver, shaking his head. 'No plants, no animals, no nothing. This desert is the driest place on earth. It never rains.'

'Never?'

'Never.'

Harrison felt his ears pop. The taxi crested the top of a hill and an enormous, dry valley opened out before them. A tall, dark mountain loomed at the other side of it, and at its summit was a flash of silver.

'There she is,' said the taxi driver. 'Mount Paranal. That's the telescope on top.'

Harrison felt the hair on his neck stand on end. Finally, here it was: the place he had travelled halfway across the world to get to. He felt excited, scared and determined, all at the same time.

As they drew closer to the mountain, Harrison realised that the flash of silver belonged to four giant silver cylinders. He pulled Shelley's postcard from his pocket: the picture on the front was exactly the same. Part way up the mountain was a cluster of large white buildings, and directly ahead of them was a huge security barrier.

Shelley must be in there somewhere, thought Harrison. *But where?*

'You want the living quarters, right?' asked the taxi driver. 'I usually take people through security and drop them there.' He glanced at Harrison in the rear-view mirror. 'That's if they've got the right papers.'

'And if they don't?' asked Harrison, in a higher voice than he had intended.

The taxi driver shrugged. 'Then I drive them back again.'

Harrison suddenly felt much more scared than he did excited or determined. What if the security guards wouldn't let him in?

'Actually,' he said suddenly. 'Why don't you let me out here? I can walk the rest of the way.'

'Whatever you say,' said the taxi driver, and skidded the car to a halt.

Harrison counted out sixty dollars. But as

he handed over the money, the taxi driver gripped his hand and looked him right in the eye.

'What's your name?' he growled. Harrison told him.

'You're not thirteen,' he said, narrowing his eyes. 'You're like, maybe, eight, nine, at the most.'

Harrison gulped. Was he about to get found out?

'So, what are you doing here? Really?' the taxi driver pressed.

Time was ticking, so Harrison decided to tell the truth.

'I've come to get my parents out of a black hole,' he said.

There was a long silence, while the taxi driver ran his tongue around his teeth, his eyes twitching with thought.

'I put my parents in a black hole too,' he said.

'Really?' asked Harrison.

'When I was young, I did some bad things. My parents found out and reported me to the police. I went to prison. For a long time, I was mad at them. Didn't speak to them, see them.' He looked Harrison in the eye. 'I put them in a black hole.'

'And what happened?' asked Harrison. 'Did you manage to get them out again?'

'No,' said the taxi driver. 'By the time I forgave them, it was too late.'

'Oh,' said Harrison. That didn't seem like a very happy end to the story.

'Don't make the same mistake I did,' said the taxi driver earnestly, twisting in his seat so they were face to face. 'Let them out before it's too late.'

'That's why I'm here,' said Harrison, not entirely sure that he and the taxi driver understood each other. 'There's someone who can help me.'

'Good,' said the taxi driver. 'I found someone like that. After I left prison. A priest.'

Now Harrison was absolutely sure they didn't understand one another.

'I'm looking for an astronomer,' he said. 'She's called Shelley.'

'Whatever it takes, little man, whatever it takes.'

There was a long pause while the taxi driver looked out at the desert and Harrison wondered how he was going to get through the gate.

'Eduardo, the security guard? He'll never let you in without papers,' said the taxi driver. 'Fact.'

'But I haven't got any papers,' admitted Harrison.

'Then you'd better get in the trunk,' said the taxi driver.

Harrison had never been in the trunk of a Chilean taxi for any length of time before, and there was very little about the experience that he ever wished to repeat. Luckily, thanks to a very large dent, the hood didn't shut properly and there was a crack just big enough for him to peep out of. At first, all he could see was red sand, but then the taxi slowed to a halt and he glimpsed a pair of black polished boots that he assumed must belong to Eduardo, the security guard the taxi driver had told him about.

The car stopped and Harrison heard the taxi driver and Eduardo having a conversation in Spanish. Harrison held his breath, hoping for the best . . . then the car started moving again. Through the crack, Harrison saw the security gate closing and Eduardo returning to his hut. They were in!

The next thing Harrison knew, the taxi driver was helping him out into blinding sunlight. On one side of the road were the large white buildings that he had seen from the entrance; on the other was a huge glass dome.

'That's where everyone lives.'

'Really?' asked Harrison, as he untied his black hole from the door handle. It had shrunk even more, and was now barely the size of an orange. 'It looks very empty.'

'That's the roof,' replied the taxi driver. 'It's all underground. If your astronomer Shelley is here, that's where you'll find her. Good luck. Can I give you some advice?'

'Yes?'

'Trust the process.'

And with that confusing sentence, he disappeared in a cloud of red dust.

There was no time to lose. Harrison took a firm grip of his black hole and headed into the building. Two smoked-glass doors slid open and he found himself on a huge balcony, looking out over an enormous swimming pool, under a domed roof that was crowded with giant palms and tropical plants.

'Can I help you, sir?'

Harrison turned to see a very official-looking lady, standing behind a high reception desk.

'I'm looking for Shelley,' said Harrison, in his loudest, clearest and bravest voice.

'I see,' said the receptionist. 'Shelley who?'

'Um, I don't know, exactly,' said Harrison. 'But she's got pink hair and she sent me this.'

He handed her Shelley's postcard.

'So, Shelley is a friend of yours . . . ?' said the receptionist, looking it over.

'She's sort of my enemy,' said Harrison, taking the postcard back and tucking it safely in his pocket. 'She gave me this black hole, which was fun at first, but has actually turned out to be quite a lot of trouble.'

The receptionist gave him a hard look, then nodded and reached for a telephone on her desk. '*Hola*, I have a young man here and I think I might need your assistance . . . *Si* . . . *Si* . . . He's looking for someone . . . He says they're his enemy.' She glanced up at Harrison and smiled. 'Yes, I think you'd better. *Gracias*, Eduardo.'

Harrison's blood ran cold. Eduardo was the security guard! The receptionist had told on him!

'Thank you, sir. If you'd like to take a seat, someone will be with you very shortly,' she said, indicating a nearby sofa.

'Thank you very much indeed,' said Harrison, keeping his cool and thinking quickly. 'I don't suppose I could use the bathroom?'

'Yes, of course,' she said. 'It's just along the corridor.'

'Thank you,' said Harrison. 'I'll be right back.'

But of course he wasn't. As he reached the door to the toilet, he heard raised voices in a room further along the corridor. He glanced back to make sure the receptionist wasn't looking, then he rushed headlong into what turned out to be a canteen.

His heart leapt! It was crowded with scientists of all shapes and sizes.

Shelley has to be here somewhere, he thought.

There was a long queue at the serving counter and tables full of laughter and chatter, but Harrison couldn't see any sign of Shelley's pink hair. There were chalkboards dotted around the room and a bearded man was in full flow, drawing a picture of what looked like an upside-down mountain.

'Excuse me,' said Harrison. 'Have you seen Shelley?'

'Who?' asked the bearded man.

'Shelley,' said Harrison. 'She's an astronomer.'

The other people round the table laughed.

'We're all astronomers here, young man,' said the bearded man.

'She's got pink hair,' tried Harrison. 'And she makes black holes. Like this one.' He jiggled the string he was holding and the black hole bobbed in the air.

'Don't be ridiculous,' said the bearded man. 'You can't carry a black hole around with you.'

The people round the table laughed again.

'Yes, you can,' said Harrison, with a steely look in his eye. And he picked up the bearded man's lunch and flipped it into his black hole. The group of scientists watched open-mouthed as the plate flew in an arc, spinning over and over, until it struck the black hole, froze and then folded into the darkness.

The bearded man raised his hands, as if Harrison was holding a loaded shotgun.

'Woah,' he murmured.

'See. It's a black hole,' said Harrison. 'Now where's Shelley?'

He glanced back down the hall and saw, to his horror, that Eduardo was at the reception desk! The receptionist pointed, and Eduardo began to walk towards them . . .

'Tell me where Shelley is!' shouted

Harrison, panicking now. 'Or I'll send every single one of you to the deepest depths of the universe!'

'We don't know!' said a long-haired man. 'We've never even heard of a Shelley working here.'

Eduardo was checking the toilets. Harrison only had seconds left.

'Not good enough!' he shouted, tossing a carton of fruit juice into the black hole.

'You could check the board!' called out a tall blonde lady. 'In the main lab, across the street. There's a big wall with everyone's photo on it!'

'Finally! Thank you!' said Harrison. At that very moment Eduardo emerged from the lavatories, caught sight of him and started towards him.

Harrison scanned the room. There was no way out except the corridor, which was now blocked by Eduardo. Then he spotted a kitchen porter pushing a trolley stacked with dirty trays towards a pair of swing doors. Harrison took off like a coursing hare, weaving his way between the tables, and bolted through the doors, only to be half-blinded by a billow of steam.

When it cleared, he found himself face to face with a rather angry-looking chef holding a huge spoonful of spaghetti. But there was no time to apologise; Eduardo was hot on his heels. A second set of swing doors beckoned at the opposite end of the kitchen and Harrison began to zigzag towards them, his black hole swishing behind him, swallowing pots and pans and chefs' hats and trays of lasagne, while the staff in the kitchen cried out and threw their arms up in confusion!

He flung himself through the doors and found himself at the bottom of a long, sloping walkway filled with bins, which led up to a third pair of swing doors with – joy of joys!

— a sliver of daylight behind them. Harrison sprinted up the slope towards them. He heard a crash behind him and looked round to see an up-turned bin, with Eduardo next to it, clawing spaghetti out of his eyes.

That gave Harrison an idea. Using all his strength, he capsized the nearest bin, so that it tumbled over onto the walkway, blocking Eduardo's path. Then he barged through the last set of swing doors and found himself outside again, looking out across red cliffs towards a dark blue ocean. Spinning on his heels, he saw a road and beyond that a large white building that he very much hoped was the main lab the blonde lady had told him about.

With his goal in sight and Eduardo in hot pursuit, Harrison tried to pick up the pace.

That was when he started to feel a bit strange. With every stride, his legs got heavier. By the time he reached the road, he had slowed to a jog, and when he reached the pathway to the laboratory, he was waddling as if his ankles were chained together. Struggling for breath, Harrison mustered every last ounce of energy and pushed through a large glass revolving door.

To his relief, the interior was cool and airy. Harrison put his hands on his knees, panting. What was happening to him? Was he ill?

'Hello again, young man.'

Harrison looked up and saw the bearded man smiling back at him. He was surrounded by other scientists, including the long-haired man, looking serious, and the tall blonde lady, raising one eyebrow.

Behind the scientists, Harrison took in a wall covered in photographs of what were obviously scientists from across the globe doing their best to look as intelligent as possible. But as he scanned the pictures, there was something wrong. Not one of them had pink hair or a scowl. In other words, not one of them was Shelley.

To make matters worse, the entire wall suddenly began to ripple, as if every face was a reflection. Then everything else started to ripple too: the pot plants either side of the doorway, Harrison's own hands as he held them in front of his face, and Eduardo as he pushed his way through the revolving door.

And that was when Harrison fainted.

Harrison opened his eyes. A spaceship had landed on the underside of a creamy-coloured planet and its green communication light was flashing.

Or at least, that's what he thought to begin with. Until he realised he was lying on his back in bed, staring at a smoke detector on the ceiling.

'Ah, you're awake,' said a voice. Harrison turned to find a doctor sitting beside him. She was making notes on a clipboard. 'How do you feel?'

'Good,' said Harrison, except that there appeared to be a mask covering his nose and mouth, so it came out funny.

The doctor plumped up the pillows and helped him to sit. Now he was more awake, Harrison took in his surroundings. He seemed to be in a very small room with just a bed and a few other pieces of basic furniture. He must have been asleep for a while because there was a tiny window looking onto the cliffs, and he could see that it was now dark outside.

The doctor put a stethoscope in her ears and put the metal bit on his chest.

'Take a deep breath,' she instructed. Harrison did as he was told and the doctor wrote something on her clipboard, then slid a rubber armband up past his elbow, pumped it up and let it slowly deflate. Then she wrote on her clipboard again. 'I think we can take that off now,' she said, lowering the mask so it was round Harrison's neck.

'Am I dying?' asked Harrison.

'No,' said the doctor, with a smile. 'You're

going to be fine.'

Harrison didn't look convinced.

'The higher up you go – and this observatory is pretty high – the less oxygen there is, which means the harder it becomes to breathe. And if you go running around, like you did –' she gave Harrison a stern look – 'then you can get something called altitude sickness. Basically, you felt sick and then fainted because you're so high up. So, it's very important that we get you back down the mountain as soon as possible. I'm assuming you're here with your parents?'

'Yes,' said Harrison, looking around for his black hole. It was tied to the bed frame. 'They're in there,' he told the doctor, pointing at the hole. It had been so long since he put anything inside it that it had now shrunk to the size of a satsuma.

'I'm sorry?'

'They're in that black hole,' said Harrison. 'What's left of it, anyway. I'm trying to get them out. But the only person who can help me is Shelley, and I can't find her.'

'Hmmm. I think you're still a little bit confused,' the doctor said, packing away her stethoscope. 'Let's pop you back on the oxygen.'

She slipped the mask over Harrison's nose and mouth and twisted the top of a small silver bottle about the size of a can of drink. Harrison could taste the oxygen now: a kind of mixture of sweet and sour that reminded him of the fizzy snake sweets he liked so much.

'I'm going to get you some more oxygen,'

the doctor said. 'Then we'll get you down the mountain and find your parents.'

'But—' Harrison started.

'No buts. You must stay here and rest,' said the doctor firmly. 'And on no account are you allowed to go any higher. That could be really bad for you.'

With that, she left the room, pulling the door shut behind her. Harrison sighed and looked at the black hole. The canteen food and pots and pans had helped, but if he didn't feed it something more soon, it would keep shrinking, until it was the size of a conker, then a marble, then a pea . . . What if it disappeared altogether? He would never be able to get his parents back.

He had come all this way, but he'd failed. What was he going to do?

He let out another sigh, lay back and closed his eyes. He missed his parents so much. Getting rid of everything he didn't like had been so much fun at first, but what was the point of being able to do exactly what you wanted if it meant you didn't have anyone to love you?

He could feel tears coming, when there was a knock at the door.

'Housekeeping,' said a voice.

The door opened and a cleaning cart came into view. It was being pushed by a familiar-looking young woman with pink hair. She smiled at Harrison, took a toilet roll off the cart and went into the bathroom. Then she backed out of the bathroom slowly, still holding the toilet roll.

'Harrison?' she asked in disbelief.

Chapter Fourteen

'Shelley?' asked Harrison, but with his oxygen mask on it sounded more like, *Shahwah?*

'How did you find me?' she said.

Harrison held up the postcard.

'You came all this way?' asked Shelley, picking up a mop from the cleaning cart. 'Why?'

Harrison pulled down the mask so that it was dangling round his neck.

'My parents,' he replied. 'I put them in the black hole. And now I want them back.'

Shelley nodded, as if she understood. Then the strangest thing happened. She sprang forward and jabbed Harrison in the chest with the mop.

'Leave me alone!' she yelled.

'*Eurgghh!*' shouted Harrison. Once again, he found himself flat on the bed, staring at the smoke detector. By the time he managed to sit up again, the door was banging shut and Shelley had gone.

What was wrong with her? Why didn't she want to help? Harrison couldn't make any sense of it.

He had to catch her. He swung his legs onto

the floor and tried to stand. It wasn't easy. Using the bed frame for support, he untied his black hole, then hobbled as quickly as he could after her.

His room was in the middle of a long green corridor, which had a door at either end. The door to his left was swinging, as if Shelley had just barged through it. So, with the oxygen bottle in one hand and his black hole in the other, he shuffled as fast as he could towards it. On the other side was a concrete staircase. He hauled himself up it, then staggered out into the open air.

He looked up. His family had once gone on holiday to the Lake District, where the stars were very bright, but this was on a whole other level. There was no moon and no clouds, and the Milky Way seemed to take up the whole sky, as if a giant had dipped a paintbrush in a bucket of stars and swept it right across the sky. For a moment, Harrison struggled to remember what it reminded him of, and then it came to him: the ceiling Shelley had created at Hector Broom's birthday party!

Shelley! There was no time to waste. Which way had she gone?

He hobbled up a path to the corner of the building, but Shelley had vanished. Could she have tricked him in the green corridor by pushing the door and running the other way? Then his eye was drawn by two tiny red lights, halfway up the mountain.

Two tiny red lights that were moving!

He squinted to try and see better. The lights belonged to a buggy that Shelley was driving at full speed up towards the telescope. Where had she got that from? Wait! Outside the main laboratory was another empty buggy!

The ground beneath him began to wobble as if it was made of jelly, and for a horrible moment, he thought he was going to be sick. The altitude sickness was striking again! Quickly, he fumbled for the oxygen mask and twisted the top of the bottle, breathing in deeply. Sweet and sour. Sweet and sour.

That did the trick. He twisted the bottle shut and pulled down the mask. Then he took a firm hold of the black hole (which was now barely the size of a plum and seemed to be getting smaller by the minute) and strode towards the buggy. This was his only chance to catch Shelley and get everything out of the black hole. No matter how heavy his legs felt, he had to keep moving.

Luckily, Harrison was no stranger to powered vehicles. His father's friend Chris the farmer had let him loose in his fields in:

1. A quad bike (which is like a motorbike with four wheels)
2. A Polaris (which is like a quad bike except it has a roof)
3. An old Land Rover
4. A tractor when it was ploughing time

So, he was sure that driving a buggy would be a piece of cake. But once he had anchored his black hole to the rear bumper and settled himself behind the wheel, he realised that every single time before, Chris the farmer had been sitting next to him, starting the engine, working the pedals and generally egging him on. He had never, ever driven a vehicle on his own, let alone on a road, and definitely not up the side of a very steep mountain while he chased a pink-haired astronomer . . .

But now wasn't the time to panic. First, he had to figure out how to start the engine. Chris always turned some sort of key, just beside the steering wheel. All there seemed to be here was a red button. Could that be it?

Harrison pressed it and the cart made a tiny lurch forward, like a racehorse champing at the bit. He slid forward on his seat and put his foot on the smaller of the two pedals. For a split-second, nothing happened, then the cart took off!

Harrison felt a wave of dizziness and clung tightly to the steering wheel as he lumped and bumped across rough terrain onto the tarmac. The road beneath him became steeper and steeper, and soon Harrison was climbing high above the desert, the wind in his hair and a giant sky full of dazzling stars.

As the buggy reached the summit, the four giant telescopes sprang into view, towering way above everything else.

The brake! He needed to find the brake! Taking a chance, he slammed his foot on the big pedal. The cart screeched to a halt, just centimetres from a concrete wall, throwing him chest-first onto the steering wheel. Phew!

There was nowhere else to hide, so Shelley must be in one of the telescopes. But which one?

He unhitched his black hole, ran to the nearest door and opened it. About half a dozen scientists turned round to look at him in surprise.

'Sorry! Wrong telescope!' said Harrison, and shut the door.

That was when he saw that the furthest telescope had a bright yellow plastic sign propped up outside it. He sprinted over to it. It read:

CLEANING IN PROGRESS
DO NOT ENTER!

Harrison took a deep breath and pushed open the door.

It was so dark inside that it took his eyes a few seconds to adjust. In the middle of the room was a huge, curved mirror, the shape of a giant half-coconut shell, pointing towards a large circular hole in the roof. Beside it was a monstrous wooden contraption that reminded Harrison of the catapults they used in olden times to fire things over the walls of castles. Together, the two things made the strangest combination: the past and the future, side by side.

Suddenly, a bright blue laser beam sprang from the roof, into the mirror and out into the night sky.

'Isn't she beautiful?' Harrison heard Shelley say from somewhere in the darkness. 'She's called Alekto and she's a Megawatt Laser. I built her myself. Here's her sister, Megaera!'

A second blue beam collided with the mirror and raced off into space.

'And, finally, meet Tisiphone!' A third blue bolt shot into the mirror, collided with her two sisters, then headed to the stars. In the place where all three beams met, sparks began to fly, and Harrison watched as a tiny black hole started to form.

'I named them after the three Furies,' announced Shelley, stepping into the light. 'Have you heard of them?'

'No,' said Harrison.

'They were from Ancient Greece,' said Shelley. 'They always got their revenge. This black hole will be mine!'

'I don't know what that means,' said Harrison.

'It means I'm leaving,' said Shelley. 'Before you or anyone else tries to stop me!'

'But I don't want to stop you!' shouted

Harrison, feeling frustrated. 'I JUST WANT MY PARENTS BACK!'

'*SSSSHHHH!*' rasped Shelley. 'Someone will hear you!'

'BUT I'M ANGRY!!!' shouted Harrison, his rage starting to take over.

'HAVEN'T YOU LEARNT ANYTHING?' shouted Shelley, even more loudly.

Harrison took a deep breath and then another. If he wanted Shelley to help him, then he knew he had to calm down.

'Please, Shelley. I put my parents in the black hole, along with lots of other things I shouldn't have,' he said, keeping his voice as steady as he could. 'But now I need to get them back. I can't look after my little sister on my own and I really miss my parents. And the Hardwicks miss Blue – or at least they did until they got sucked into the black hole too. And even Hector Broom has someone who misses him! Please can you show me how to get out the things that I put in?'

Shelley's expression changed from outrage to surprise.

'Wow!' she said. 'That's really impressive.'

'What is?' asked Harrison in between breaths.

'It's worked!'

Harrison still didn't understand.

'I gave you that black hole to help you control your temper, because you behaved so badly at the party,' said Shelley.

'Really?' asked Harrison.

'Yes. And look at you now. Using your words instead of Kicking Off!' said Shelley. Then her voice softened. 'Listen, Harrison, anger can be good. Important, even. *I'm* angry. But it's about what you do with your anger. I don't *lose* my temper, I *use* it.'

She placed a hand on Harrison's shoulder and he looked up into her sharp green eyes.

'When I was your age, I wanted to study science. And I wasn't allowed to because I was a girl. That made me angry. But instead of kicking and screaming and shouting, I used my anger to build this . . . an Einstein-Rosen bridge, so I could travel to the future and become an astronomer!'

'Like your grandmother,' said Harrison helpfully.

'Excuse me?' asked Shelley, not quite understanding.

'She built a . . . Steinway-Moses . . . One of these things too.'

'You really don't know who I am, do you?' asked Shelley.

'Of course I do,' replied Harrison hesitantly. 'You're Shelley.'

'I'll give you a clue: Garibaldi.'

Shelley fished in her pocket and pulled out a half-eaten biscuit.

'About thirty seconds after I arrived, this hit me right in the back of my neck,' explained Shelley, handing it over. 'I think it belongs to your sister.'

For a moment, Harrison couldn't even begin to understand what Shelley meant. Then, suddenly, he realised what she was trying to tell him . . .

'The postcard said: "To Shelley" and "From Shelley",' he said slowly.

'That's right,' said Shelley, with an

encouraging smile.

'And your grandmother told me about looking at parents and grandparents to see what we would look like when we were older . . . '

'Yes,' nodded Shelley.

'Which means . . . ' Harrison gasped.

'That old lady isn't my grandmother. It's me!' Shelley finished for him.

And then everything went dark.

Chapter Fifteen

'Harrison! Harrison!'

Someone far, far away was calling him.

'Harrison, wake up!'

He opened his eyes and immediately felt sick. How much of that was to do with altitude and how much to do with Shelley shaking him vigorously by the shoulders, he wasn't exactly sure.

'What happened?' he asked her.

'You fainted,' said Shelley. 'I was going to give you some oxygen, but then I figured you might need it. Because this needs feeding.'

She held up what appeared to be an empty piece of string, hovering in mid-air.

'It's gone!' exclaimed Harrison.

'Almost,' said Shelley. 'It's about the size of a strawberry seed. I'd say you've got another —' she made some quick calculations in her head — 'five minutes and thirty-eight seconds before it disappears altogether.'

'What?' exclaimed Harrison.

'We need to move fast,' said Shelley, 'so I'm going to keep this short. Number one: you need to put the entire earth in your black hole. That's the only thing that can stop it shrinking to nothing now. Number two: you need to make it spin. Number three: you need to throw yourself into it. Am I making sense?'

'Not really,' said Harrison.

'Okay,' said Shelley. 'There's no way out of a black hole, *unless* it's spinning.' She pressed a button on a remote, and the giant mirror began to rotate. 'Because, as you know, that turns the black hole into an Einstein-Rosen bridge . . .'

As she spoke, she climbed the rickety wooden contraption, into a seat that was set on top of a giant lever arm.

'But I need your help!' called Harrison over the noise of the machine. 'I still don't know how to get everything back!'

'You'll be fine,' said Shelley, bracing

herself. 'It's pretty much foolproof. Just remember: Earth, Spin, Throw Yourself In.' She pressed another button on the remote. 'Oh, wait,' she said. 'There's one more thing I need to tell you. Make sure the black hole is spinning the right way. Last time I did this, I went into the past instead of the future!'

'Lift-off in T minus

ten . . . nine . . . eight . . .'

boomed a voice.

Shelley settled back in her seat, ready for another extraordinary journey!

'Seven . . . six . . .'

'One more thing,' she said, breaking her concentration for a moment.

'Five . . . four . . . ,

'You've got to get the speed right. I wasn't quite fast enough and ended up twenty-eight instead of eight! You don't want to change age, so creep in as slowly as possible!'

'Three . . . two . . . ,

She gave Harrison a big smile, and sat back again.

Then a split-second later, she sat back up.

'One . . . '

'And you need to keep calm!' she shouted. 'Any emotional disturbance and you'll end up off your timeline.'

'Ignition!'

'Which means there'll be two of you – the new you and the old you! And, trust me, you really don't want that!'

The mirror was now spinning really fast and the noise was almost deafening.

'Blast off!'

'Apart from that, it's quite literally child's plaaaaaaaaaay!'

The giant arm launched her head-first across the room, right into the spinning black hole!

All that was left were the soles of Shelley's shoes, fading slowly from view . . .

But Harrison didn't wait to watch them fade into darkness. He had work to do and very little time in which to do it.

He snatched up the string and ran outside.

He fitted his mask to his face and twisted the top of the oxygen bottle.

Sweet and sour, sweet and sour.

Then he dipped the end of the string into the dust on the ground.

Nothing.

Was he too late? He peered at the end of the string. If his black hole was there, he couldn't see it.

He tried again, dipping the bottom of the string back in the sand.

And then something started to happen.

Something incredible.

All the sand on the plateau began to tremble, as if it was being sucked up by the world's most powerful and most tiny hoover. There was a jolt and he was hit by a gale of wind, flinging him upwards.

It was as much as he could do to hold on.

Now he could see his black hole again, right at the end of the string, the size of a golf ball.

It was working! The hole was growing again!

Beneath him, the entire mountain appeared to shudder and fold, as if it was as thin as a bed sheet . . . then it sucked up into the black hole.

Harrison felt as if his head was about to explode as the wind blasted against him even more strongly!

He took a deep breath through the mask.

Sweet and sour, sweet and sour.

The black hole was the size of a football now and still growing. Way below him, the earth began to curve and the sun began to rise, as torrents of rock rushed up towards him.

For a few brief seconds, he was burning in the brightest, hottest sunlight he had ever seen!

And then he was plunged into darkness.

Sweet and sour, sweet and sour.

And suddenly he was floating in space, with nothing but a huge black hole between him and the sun.

The entire earth had disappeared inside his black hole! The whole world, and everything in it: every person, animal and plant was relying on him to get this right.

He looked at the oxygen bottle. He could only have a few minutes of oxygen left. He needed to think fast.

Sweet and sour, sweet and sour.

Shelley's words echoed in his brain. 'Earth,

Spin, Throw Yourself In.'

He'd put the earth in. Now he needed to make the black hole spin. But which way? And how?

He looked up at the black hole, deep and dark, with the sun burning round it like a halo. But wait . . . where were the stars? Ah, there they were, like a carpet beneath his feet.

Now what was it Shelley had been trying to tell him, before she shot off? Spin one way and you go into the past. Spin the other way and you go into the future.

But which was which?

There was no way to know.

He looked down at his trainers. There was a bright star, halfway between them, that he thought he recognised! Now that he looked more closely, he could see that the criss-cross pattern beneath his feet was Cygnus, the swan, and the bright star was Deneb, its tail!

But there was a problem.

Cygnus wasn't spinning. And that meant he wasn't spinning either.

He tried twisting his body. It was useless. There was nothing to push against except empty space. And then he had an idea.

He took off one of his shoes, threw it and Cygnus looked like it was beginning to turn, which meant he and his black hole were spinning.

So he took off his other shoe and threw that too.

Now Cygnus was turning even faster!

Then Harrison started to climb the string,

hand over hand, closer and closer to the black hole.

He stretched out his hand . . .

His heart began to beat faster.

What if something went wrong? What if he fell inside and never got out?

Keep calm, Shelley said.

He had to keep calm!

Sweet and sour, sweet and sour . . .

He touched its edge . . .

Then – *whoosh!* – he took off, as if he was sliding head-first down the world's biggest water slide!

Harrison was thrown left and right and up and down as he rushed through space and time, faster and faster!

He saw Blue barking . . . then a giant piece of broccoli . . . Hector Broom, flicking his elastic band . . . swimming pools and textbooks rushing past him so fast he had to close his eyes . . .

And, finally, way off in the distance, he glimpsed his parents, waving to him . . .

But, wait, were they waving hello or goodbye?

Suddenly he was rushing away from them, out past stars and galaxies and galactic clusters . . .

Out into darkness.

And then everything stopped.

Harrison opened his eyes.

There was Cygnus again. Only it wasn't spinning any more!

It hadn't worked!

Then Harrison realised he wasn't wearing his oxygen mask.

Harrison was thrown left and right, and up and down, as
he rushed through space and time.

He was lying on his back, looking up at the stars on the ceiling at Hector Broom's space party!

'Right!' said Shelley. 'Shall we play some games?' She flicked a row of switches on the wall and all the lights came back on.

He'd done it! He'd travelled back in time to Hector's birthday party! That meant none of the Bad Things had happend yet! His parents, Blue, Hector Broom and the entire planet were safe and sound!

For a few seconds, Harrison lay there, flooded with relief. Then he smiled an absolutely enormous smile. He jumped to his feet and raised his hand as high as it would go.

'Yes!' he bellowed.

And everybody laughed.

Needless to say, it turned out to be one of the best birthday parties ever. And when Hector Broom pulled out his rubber band and gave a menacing smirk, Harrison found he didn't care. Once you've seen the inside of a black hole and lost almost everyone you love, an elastic band doesn't seem quite so scary. Harrison was enjoying himself so much that he hardly noticed his mother and father creeping in at the end.

'You're here!' yelled Harrison, and raced across the room to give them both a huge hug. He'd missed his parents so much. Then he spotted Lana and gave her a huge hug too.

'Harrison has been a real pleasure to look after,' Shelley told his parents.

One by one, Shelley gave each child a slice of birthday cake and a beautiful, shiny helium balloon in the shape of a planet. Hector Broom got a stripy brown and yellow Jupiter, and Persephone Brinkwater got a purple Venus. Charlie Nwosu got a sky-blue Neptune, Marcus Down got an orange Saturn with pink rings and Carl Ng got a bluey-green Uranus. Katie Broad got a silvery Mercury, which was very lucky because it matched her angel costume.

Finally, it was Harrison's turn.

'Have you got a balloon for Harrison?' asked Harrison's mother.

'Ah,' said Shelley. 'Yes, I've got a special balloon for you, Harrison.'

Harrison's heart sank. Could it be happening all over again? He didn't want a black hole!

But then Shelley handed him a beautiful red balloon.

'This is Mars,' she said, tying it to his wrist. 'Who's "Mars" named after, do you know?'

Harrison shook his head.

'He's the Roman God of War,' said Shelley. 'But to win, he has to learn to control his temper.'

'Maybe someone should give him a black hole,' said Harrison with a knowing smile.

Epilogue

I started by saying that most stories are about a good person who does a Bad Thing, and that this story was no exception.

So let me finish by saying that most stories about a good person who does a Bad Thing have a moral, and this story is no exception to that rule either.

So what, you may ask, is the moral of this story?

Well, there are a few, really. One (which I

think Harrison would agree with) is:

Don't Kick Off at birthday parties.

Another might be this:

However difficult it is living in a world where people get angry, a world where people didn't get angry would be worse. If people didn't get angry about injustices or unfairness then things would never change.

Or maybe this:

Sometimes angry people are just frightened people in disguise.

And lastly, and perhaps most importantly:

If you bottle up your worries, they might come out as anger. But if you try to explain your worries, you might just find someone who understands, and who is able to help.

The Science Bit

Since I wrote this story, I have received lots of letters from children asking me if black holes are real, and whether there is any danger that they might accidentally fall into one.

First: the bad news. Black holes are real. There's one in the constellation of Cygnus, just like in the story, and some people even say there's a tiny one, about the size of a balloon, in the outer reaches of our solar system.

But now: the good news. The chances of falling into one are zero. Unless, that is, you are planning a holiday near Deneb, or a mini break beyond Neptune.

So what else in the story is true?

Well, Harrison is a real person, though he's never been on a mini break beyond Neptune, so he's never fallen into a black hole, or been able to put anything else into one either. (Although sometimes I'm sure he wishes he could.) And until he learnt to use his words, he really did have a temper.

Black holes do shrink, although not nearly as fast as they do in this story. The very clever scientist Stephen Hawking taught us that. And according to two other very clever scientists, Albert Einstein and Nathan Rosen, a spinning black hole might – I repeat *might* – form an Einstein-Rosen bridge, but no one has ever seen a real grandmother travel back in time through one.

The other thing in Harrison's story that is definitely real is the Very Large Telescope in the Atacama Desert. The VLT is the world's most advanced visible-light astronomical observatory – which basically means that it's the best place in the entire world to go if you want to see something in space – and is actually a collection of four telescopes. Together they are so powerful that if you took a car to the moon and turned on its headlights, the VLT would be able to see them from Earth. The observatory is open to visitors, so you can go and see it for yourself. You just need to log on to the website. And smuggle yourself onto a flight to Chile, of course.

Or become an astronomer.

Then you can see black holes for yourself. Or maybe even make one . . .

Acknowledgements

The first person I have to thank is Harrison Miller, my son, for (a) letting me write this book about him, (b) listening so attentively whenever I read bits of it to him when he would much rather be doing something else, and (c) supreme tact whenever he felt something wasn't really working. And while I'm at it, I also need to thank his older brother, Sonny, and his younger sister, Lana, who also feature and gave me lots of helpful advice.

Neither Harrison nor Lana would be here without my wonderful wife, Jessica Parker; thank you, Jess, for making our home such a transcendentally fun and loving place to be, and for listening to more guff about black holes than any soul can usefully bear.

Daniela Terrazzini is the most brilliant illustrator. Working with her has been a joyous to and fro, and her otherworldly cover – which she somehow managed to create before I'd finished the book – gave me the perfect ending.

I had the germ of this idea a while ago, and it's thanks to my luminous agent Luigi Bonomi, that it became what Harrison would call a 'chapter book'. Without Jane Griffiths, however, my gifted editor at Simon and Schuster, I very much doubt it would be worth the paper its printed on. Jane has been a pitch-perfect sounding board from the very beginning, re-structuring the story, crafting the characters, and writing all the best lines.

And while I'm thanking Jane, I must include the dazzling Rachel Denwood's amazing team at Simon and Schuster Children's: Sarah Macmillan and Eve Wersocki-Morris for their standout marketing and PR; Laura Hough for her indefatigable sales, Sophie Marchbank for her peerless production, Sally Byford for her creative copyedit; Jenny Glencross, Melissa Gitari and Sally Critchlow for their commanding proofreads; and Jenny Richards for her glorious design.

Chloe Davies and James Douglas from

Four PR have run an outstanding campaign, and my own personal publicists, Clair Dobbs and Caroline Fergusson, at CLD Communications remain my go-tos for all things public and relatable.

Thanks also to my tip-top acting agent Samira Davies, and her equally tip and equally top assistants, Lisa Stretton, Geri Spicer and Alice Burton at Independent. And a galaxy of thank yous to my erstwhile personal assistant, Tasha Brade.

I am very lucky to be on first-name terms with some thoroughly unshabby physicists, who have shared their insights on black holes over the years: special mention must go to Brian Cox, Jim Al-Khalili and Carlos Frenck. You may not know you helped, but you did. I have been a lifelong fan of Stephen Hawking, who had a heart to match his extraordinary brain, and is sorely missed.

Finally, a huge caffeinated thank you to David Hodgetts, Sezan Walker, Rafael Agrizzi L De Medeiros, Aaliyah Main, and Marcus Hayes at Triple Two Coffee. I promise to let someone else have that corner seat for a bit.

Have you read the true story of Father Christmas?

'Enchanting and funny'
Philip Ardagh

'A fire-side gem of a story'
Abi Elphinstone

'Bubbles with warmth and mischievous humour . . . irresistible'
Alexander Armstrong